"So, what is this of

"Me."

Evie's dark brows gathered in an adorable frown as she tried to work out what Griffin was saying. "Yes," she agreed, before stating, "your offer. What is it?"

"No, sweetheart, you don't understand. I'm offering you my...services."

Her jaw dropped, and it took all the strength he had not to erase the distance between them and press a kiss against her parted pink lips. He contented himself with pulling her close enough to feel the softness of her breasts against his chest and the brush of her thigh between his own.

"I'm offering to help you find a balance between your professional and personal lives." He congratulated himself on a phrasing that would appeal to Evie's logical mind.

"So we'd—what, exactly? Pretend to go out to fool my aunt into thinking I have a life?"

He couldn't help it. He laughed. "Or we could simply go out together with no subterfuge involved. Take tonight for example—hanging out at a bar, having a few drinks, dancing... This is what having a life feels like, Evie."

And yet for all the *living* he'd done during his teens and twenties, he'd never felt anything quite like holding Evie McClaren in his arms.

HILLCREST HOUSE:
Destination...romance

Dear Reader,

Christmas books will always have a special place in my heart, not only because I love to read them but because my very first Special Edition had a Christmas theme. I'm thrilled to be revisiting the most wonderful time of the year in *Their Yuletide Promise*!

From the beginning of my Hillcrest House series, no-nonsense, strictly business Evie McClaren has been hard at work in the background. Nothing is going to distract her from her goal of one day running the family hotel—certainly not a flirtatious playboy like Griffin James.

But when her aunt worries that Evie is spending too much time focusing on business, Evie comes up with the perfect plan for the holidays. All she has to do is follow the four *f*'s—family, friends, fun and falling in love—to prove to her aunt that she can run the hotel and still have a life. Burned by love in the past, Evie doesn't have any intention of actually opening her heart, but this *is* the season of miracles...

Though Evie doesn't know it, Griffin James has a plan of his own. Griffin has been intrigued by Evie since the first time they met, and if she's looking for a boyfriend to kiss beneath the mistletoe, he's the man for the job! But will an agreement that's meant to last only through the holidays ring in a New Year and new life together for Evie and Griffin?

I hope you enjoy *Their Yuletide Promise*, the final book in the Hillcrest House series. If you've missed the previous books, you can find both *The Best Man Takes a Bride* and *How to Be a Blissful Bride* online.

I always love hearing from readers at stacyconnelly@cox.net or on Facebook.

Hoping all your yuletide wishes come true!

Stacy Connelly

Their Yuletide Promise

Stacy Connelly

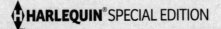

HARLEQUIN® SPECIAL EDITION

Recycling programs
for this product may
not exist in your area.

ISBN-13: 978-1-335-57416-9

Their Yuletide Promise

Copyright © 2019 by Stacy Cornell

Printed in U.S.A.

Stacy Connelly has dreamed of publishing books since writing stories about a girl and her horse. Eventually, boys made it onto the page as she discovered a love of romance novels. She is thrilled that her novel *Once Upon a Wedding* was recently turned into a movie titled *Christmas Wedding Planner*.

Stacy lives in Arizona with her two spoiled dogs. She loves to hear from readers at stacyconnelly@cox.net, at stacyconnelly.com or on Facebook.

Books by Stacy Connelly

Harlequin Special Edition

Hillcrest House

The Best Man Takes a Bride
How to Be a Blissful Bride

Furever Yours

Not Just the Girl Next Door

The Pirelli Brothers

His Secret Son
Romancing the Rancher
Small-Town Cinderella
Daddy Says, "I Do!"
Darcy and the Single Dad
Her Fill-In Fiancé

Temporary Boss...Forever Husband

Visit the Author Profile page
at Harlequin.com for more titles.

To all the Special Edition authors I've had the pleasure to meet over the years... I'm thrilled to be counted among such talented writers!

Prologue

"Are you sure you don't want me to stay?"

Evie McClaren glanced up from her computer screen, surprised to see her cousin biting her lower lip as she stood in the doorway. It was a sign Rory was worried when she had no reason to be.

"I've got this," Evie reassured her. "I've done the math." She placed a hand on the business plan she'd printed out. "With the work you've done establishing Hillcrest House as an all-inclusive wedding destination, occupancy rates—and profits—are up. Once I show Aunt E the projections, she'll forget all about selling the hotel."

Her stomach hollowed out as she said the words. *Selling Hillcrest House...* She still couldn't believe her aunt was even considering an offer from a national chain. One that would turn the unique Victorian with its floral-themed suites into a bland, carbon-copy hotel where all the rooms would look the same whether in Portland, Oregon, or Portland, Maine.

"I can't even imagine losing this place. I mean, I thought we loved it when we were kids…" Rory's voice trailed off. As young girls, they had roamed the halls of Hillcrest like it was their very own fairy-tale castle, weaving *once upon a times* and never doubting one day their princes would come. "It means even more to me now."

Rory had never lost her belief in happily-ever-after, a faith that had only grown since she'd found the love of her life. Evie was glad for her cousin. She really was. She simply didn't have time to hear about it. Again.

So before Rory could start in on how romantic it was that she'd met her now fiancé at one of the weddings she'd coordinated, or how her brother, Chance, and his bride-to-be, Alexa, had reunited right here at Hillcrest House, where the elegant hotel brought two hearts together with its blend of magic and romance and blah, blah, blah— Evie reminded Rory of an upcoming appointment with a potential bride and ushered her cousin out of the small office.

Settling back at her computer, she clicked the mouse. A slideshow of colorful graphs and charts flashed across the large monitor. Maybe she should have had the meeting in one of the hotel's larger rooms and used a projector for bigger impact.

But with her aunt arriving in five minutes, it was too late to second-guess herself. Besides, her aunt didn't want bells and whistles. Cold, hard numbers were the way to go. Evie was sure of it.

Half an hour later, Evie was no longer sure of anything.

Staring at her aunt, she sputtered, "But the numbers…" She gestured to her business plan—one that detailed the hotel's occupancy rate, the increased revenue, the growth projections for the next five years. The one her aunt had barely glanced at before setting the spiral-bound document aside.

"I know what the numbers say, hon." Reaching up, the older woman tucked a short strand of hair behind her ear. A few months after chemotherapy, Evelyn's once-color-treated auburn hair had grown back into an almost-pixie style with a wisp of silver-streaked bangs falling across her forehead.

The small sign of victory over the deadly disease filled Evie with a sense of relief and pride. Her aunt was a fighter and no one in the family was surprised that she'd beaten cancer. But Evie was still getting used to her aunt's new look…and new outlook.

Because Evelyn's hair and more casual clothes—today, a colorful broomstick skirt and peach tunic sweater—weren't the only changes. Everything about her aunt was more comfortable and relaxed. All of which made Evie feel strangely on edge.

"Running the hotel takes a level of commitment, of… sacrifice," Evelyn began.

"I know how hard you've worked all these years, but that's why my idea is so perfect. I'm ready for the challenge. This job, Hillcrest…" Though Evie reminded herself this was a business meeting and she was a professional, she couldn't help the tremor of emotion as she said, "It means everything to me."

Though she had always scoffed at her cousin's belief in the hotel's magic, Evie *had* fallen in love. She'd fallen for the history, the stability, the permanence of the gorgeous Victorian mansion.

Crunching the numbers, overseeing the staff and managing the business side of the historic hotel did more than simply satisfy her CPA brain. Her success—after public and private failures—had started to heal her broken spirit. She felt that she'd come full circle, that all the heartbreak of the past had led her back to Hillcrest House and to a future running the hotel.

Her aunt's smile was tinged with a sadness Evie recognized but didn't understand. "And that's the problem," Evelyn said.

Evie shook her head, refocusing on the logic of her argument. "No, Aunt E, there's no problem. I've done the research—"

"Evie, sweetie, I'm not talking about the research. I'm talking about you."

"Me?" *She* was the problem? There wasn't a single equation where Evie hadn't factored in turning Hillcrest House into an even bigger success. How could she be the problem? "I—I don't understand."

"You're a young woman, and it's a Saturday night. You should be out."

"Out? Out where?" With her head spinning, Evie was unable to silence the inane question. None of this made sense.

"Out with friends. Out having a good time."

"I don't have any friends here. I haven't had…"

"Time?" her aunt filled in when Evie's voice trailed away as she realized a split second too late that she was adding to, rather than subtracting from, her aunt's argument. "If this illness has taught me anything, it's that there's more to life than work. There's family and friends and falling in love."

With her thoughts still reeling, Evie had no idea what they talked about before her aunt said her goodbyes. Dropping back into her chair, she stared at her computer until the screen blurred and tears burned her vision.

Eyestrain. Nothing more than eyestrain.

Evie wasn't the emotional type. Certainly not someone who would break down and cry just because her aunt, her namesake, the woman she had admired and emulated her entire adult life, didn't think she was the right person to take over the family hotel.

And the ridiculous reason *why* her Aunt Evelyn didn't want Evie taking over? Well, that was almost enough to make her laugh.

Love?

Once upon a time, Evie had believed in love. She'd spent the past two years paying for that mistake.

The PowerPoint slide shifted, the colorful graphs and charts flashing her five-year plan across the screen and making a mockery of all her hard work. She'd built the business model step-by-step and...

Leaning forward, she reached for the mouse and hit the button to freeze the slides. She blinked a few times to clear the darn eyestrain. If there was one thing Evie knew, it was how to follow through on a plan. This time she didn't even need to formulate the steps to success. Her aunt had already given her specific instructions. If Evie wanted to take over Hillcrest House, all she needed to do was to prove to her aunt that she could run the hotel *and* have a life.

Straightening her shoulders, she rolled her chair closer to the computer and got down to business. Determination burned through her disappointment like wildfire. "I've got this," she muttered beneath her breath.

Family...friends...fun...falling in love...

How hard could it be?

Chapter One

Four weeks later, Evie realized her plan was not going to be as easy to pull off as she'd hoped. And if her aunt thought sitting in her office alone on a Saturday night was pathetic? Well, Evie had discovered something far worse.

Sitting in a bar alone on a Saturday night.

As she stared at the bottom of her martini glass, ignoring the conversation and laughter ringing out all around her, Evie had to give herself a little bit of credit. She had actually made some progress on the first three items of what she was calling her 4-F plan.

Evie had made sure she attended the McClaren family Thanksgiving gathering though leaving the office hadn't been easy. After all, she'd had inventory to reconcile, monthly invoices to review, financials to prepare for the upcoming year-end audit.

Even so, she'd been only half an hour late to dinner. And she had made sure to keep her phone on Vibrate during the meal, though she had needed to excuse herself a few times during dessert to take calls from the hotel staff.

On the friends front, she'd gone shopping on Black Friday with Rory and, well, Rory's friends. How her cousin had already forged such strong ties baffled Evie, but the other women had welcomed her warmly even though she was well aware she was leeching off her cousin's friendships.

She might have even had fun, ticking off the third item, had her single status not become more and more apparent as the women shopped for their significant others. Evie had no one special to shop for and, standing around in the men's section, listening to their romantic plans for the upcoming holidays, that final F—falling in love— had never seemed more out of reach.

Which brought a fifth F to mind.

Failure.

Evie shoved the thought from her mind. She would not fail. Not this time. Not that she had any intention of actually falling in love.

Pressure filled her chest, and Evie sucked in a deep breath to keep the unwanted, messy mix of emotions from exploding. All she needed to do was prove to her aunt that she was putting herself out there. That she was spending time with family and friends and…dating.

That was the goal Evie had set for herself: securing a date for both her cousin Chance's Christmas Eve wedding to Alexa Mayhew and the upcoming New Year's Eve Ball. Her aunt would be on hand for both events, and Evie would not—could not—go alone.

She had the perfect plan. Now she needed the perfect man.

But with the wedding a week away, Evie was no closer to finding a date than she was to finding a magical unicorn.

And instead of embracing the holiday spirit, she felt far more like the Grinch trying to find a way to keep Christmas from coming.

Honestly, did people actually enjoy doing this kind of thing?

Not that she'd intended to be sitting alone in a bar on a Saturday night. She was supposed to be on a second date with a guy she'd met online. Only he'd canceled at the last minute. Evie couldn't blame him. She'd delayed their initial coffee date twice and then an emergency at the hotel had called her back before her espresso had cooled enough for her to take more than a single sip. This time, a problem with his own business had forced Wade to no-show. Evie supposed that was what she got for trying to find a man too similar to herself.

Maybe she needed to look for someone who was a little less of a workaholic. Someone a little more…fun.

Evie was in the right place for it. Clearville's Bar and Grille was decked out for the holidays with an odd mix of wreaths and garlands hung amid the neon beer signs. Rock-and-roll Christmas carols blasted from the jukebox. Groups of men and women filled the high-top tables and the length of the bar. The appetizers ordered by the couples on either side of her were typical bar food; the scent of the battered onion rings and buffalo wings alone was probably enough to clog her arteries. But the drinks…

Evie tipped back the wide sugarcoated rim of her glass, somewhat surprised to find herself down to her last swallow of the candy-cane-garnished peppermint martini. She waved to capture the bartender's attention.

"It's happy hour," he announced over the loud music as he set two empty glasses in front of her. "Two for one."

"Perfect," she muttered. Even drinks came in pairs nowadays.

A loud cheer rose from the crowd gathered around the garish garland-draped pool table, and Evie glanced across the bar. High fives and money were exchanged as one of the players was declared a winner.

"Time to put your money where your mouth is, Travis! The guy ran the table on you!" one of the bystanders announced as he took the pool cue from his dark-haired friend.

The man, Travis, handed over a wad of cash. "Next time we'll find a more interesting wager."

"Name it," the winner challenged, holding up the bills. "Your money's on me."

A shiver raced down Evie's spine at the sound of that deep, slightly amused, slightly arrogant voice. She leaned to one side of the bar stool, gasping when she almost toppled over. Jeez, how strong did they make these martinis? Bracing a hand on the edge of the bar, she tried to get a better look at the trio.

She recognized the dark-haired Travis and his blond friend as locals, but the third man in the group, standing with his back to Evie, was the one who caught her attention. His thick golden-brown hair gleamed even in the bar's dim atmosphere. Broad shoulders stretched the limits of a pale blue tailored shirt, the sleeves rolled back to reveal leanly muscled forearms.

One hand held a pool cue with a confident ease that had Evie thinking of Paul Newman in that old black-and-white movie. He tucked the wad of cash into his pocket with his other hand, the material of his slate-gray trousers pulling tight against a perfectly formed backside.

Her mouth went dry and she struggled to swallow.

It almost sounded like… Almost looked like… But it wouldn't be…couldn't be…

Evie jumped, nearly losing her balance once again, startled by a loud clatter. Ice rattled around in a stainless steel shaker as the bartender mixed her martinis before straining the chilled concoction into the two glasses. Her heart still pounding, she refused his offer of a menu and glanced back across the bar. The Clearville locals had taken over the pool table, and the third man was gone.

She had to be imagining things. No way would *Griffin James*, heir to the James Hotels empire, be hustling pool in tiny Clearville. A childhood friend of Alexa's, he *was* coming into town for her wedding, though Alexa had been somewhat vague about when. Griffin wasn't the type to abide by schedules, something made easier by the wealth that afforded him not only a pilot's license but his own private plane, as well.

Evie pushed all thoughts of Griffin James from her mind. She had a sound, logical plan to put into motion, and for that plan to work, she needed a sound, logical man. Someone who would fit into the equation with comfort and ease. No messy complications. No unwanted surprises. No uncontrolled mix of emotions.

That sound, logical plan didn't stop her from glancing toward the pool table again, hoping to catch another glimpse of the man who wouldn't be—couldn't be—the same one she absolutely had not been thinking about since his stay at Hillcrest House almost two months ago.

Because Griffin James was not standing by the pool table.

"For me?" As the deep—and familiar—voice murmured in her ear, Evie realized he was, in fact, standing right behind her.

A masculine arm reached around her, and she caught

sight of pale blue material rolled back to reveal tanned skin dusted with dark blond hair. He claimed one of the martinis, his palm cupping the delicate glass, and Evie's mouth went dry. "I'm really more of a beer kind of guy, but I never refuse when a lady offers me a drink."

"I didn't offer, and I don't believe you." The words popped out before she could stop them, a bad habit made worse when she was nervous. But she wasn't about to let him know he had that effect—any effect—on her.

With that thought in mind, she turned. And found herself staring at a patch of skin exposed by the open collar of his shirt. At five-eight plus heels, Evie was accustomed to looking a man in the eye—if not literally looking down on him. But not this man.

She had to look up beyond that tempting triangle of skin, up the strong column of his neck, past the cleft in his chin where her attention snagged on his confident smile and the sexy mouth inches from her own. Heat suffused her body, and the pounding of her heart matched the pounding in her ears as the music switched to Bruce Springsteen's "Santa Claus Is Coming to Town."

But the only words Evie could hear were her aunt's. *You've locked yourself away from the world at a time when you should be out living your life instead of letting it pass you by...*

Evie didn't want to admit her aunt was right about, well, any of the reasons why she shouldn't be the one to run the hotel. But maybe her moratorium on the opposite sex had gone on for too long if she'd lost her ability to handle a ridiculous charmer like Griffin James.

Evie didn't do charm.

And yet Griffin didn't appear the least bit discouraged by her outburst. "You don't believe...?"

"I don't believe beer is your drink of choice. You probably bathe in champagne."

White teeth flashed in a quick smile. "Imagining me naked again, Ms. McClaren?"

"No, not again." Catching the knowing arch in his brow, she belatedly recognized her slip. Flustered, she amended, "Not—not even in the first place."

"Are you sure? Because I specifically recall you trying to take my clothes off the night we met."

The night they'd met, Chance and Griffin had gotten in a fight over Alexa, who—at the time—had been *Griffin's* fiancée.

Raising her chin, she said, "I offered to have your shirt sent to the cleaners after you so thoughtlessly bled on the silk. You really shouldn't have such nice things if you aren't going to take care of them."

"I promise you, Evie…" Despite the din surrounding them, his deep voice wrapped around her, all warmth and seduction melting her from the inside out. And if that wasn't enough to sway her under his spell, he reached up and trailed a fingertip across her cheek as he brushed a lock of hair back from her face. "I take very good care of the fine things in my hands."

The light touch sent shivers racing over her skin. Such a small taste of what those hands could do if Griffin really put his mind to it. But a split second before Evie would have ducked and run, Griffin stepped back and lifted his—her—glass. His attitude once more laid-back and casual, he offered a friendly, flirty wink. "You might as well admit it. You were worried about me…and wanted to see me with my shirt off."

The lighthearted teasing put them back on even ground, and Evie sucked in a quick breath. Good grief!

Overreact much? So what if Griffin was flirting? That was what Griffin James did.

"If I was worried, it was that you might sue the hotel after my cousin beat you up. And speaking of Chance..." Recalling a pop-up from the calendar app that ruled her life, she asked, "Isn't his bachelor party tonight? Shouldn't you be hanging out with the guys?"

Griffin smirked a little. "I wasn't invited to Chance's party."

"I can't imagine why not."

"I thought about crashing, but like you said, it's just a bunch of guys hanging out. What's the fun in that?" He flashed a devilish smile as he added, "I think maybe I'll show up for Alexa's party tomorrow instead."

He was kidding. He had to be kidding. "You do that, and this time my cousin might kill you."

"I'm not afraid of Chance."

"Who said anything about Chance? You ruin the bridal shower, and Rory will be the one you'll have to watch out for."

"Ah, yes, Hillcrest House's wedding planner extraordinaire."

Of course, Griffin would know who Rory was. After all, she'd taken him on a tour of the hotel—when Griffin and Alexa had been the ones thinking of getting married.

Not that he seemed particularly distraught over his broken engagement, Evie mused, as she reached for her own drink and eyed him over the sugared rim. A slightly mocking smile tilted his too-tempting lips, but something in his eyes—something a little envious, a little lonely?— grabbed hold of Evie.

After all, Griffin wasn't the only one whose wedding plans had stopped a few yards short of a walk down the aisle.

"Rory explained all about Hillcrest's promise of happily-ever-after. How it's a place where two hearts come together to find a lasting love." His eyebrows rose at the disbelieving snort she couldn't quite silence. "You don't believe it?"

"You're telling me you do? Even after Alexa dumped you?" Evie regretted the words she'd blurted out the second they left her mouth. "Sorry, I shouldn't have—"

"What? Told it like it is? Don't apologize for that." He leaned forward to set his glass on the bar, erasing the slight distance she'd put between them. "It's one of the things I like best about you, Evie."

She wasn't sure she'd ever met anyone who actually *liked* how outspoken she was. And that was only *one* of the things? As in, there was more about her that he liked? Tipsy butterflies took flight in her stomach, and even though Evie wanted to roll her eyes and dismiss the whole idea, she couldn't manage to pull her gaze away from his.

And what was it he'd asked her? Oh, right. About the hotel. About happily-ever-after. But she didn't dare let herself be distracted. Not when there was so much at stake. Not when *Hillcrest House* was at stake. She had to focus on her plan. If only she wasn't starting to feel like she'd need a Christmas miracle to pull it off.

"Happily-ever-after is Rory's forte. She's Hillcrest's heart. I'm the brains of the operation." She cringed a little. "Not that Rory isn't smart. I'm just—"

"Smarter?" Griffin supplied, tongue in cheek.

Lifting her martini for another drink, she muttered, "Better with numbers than with people. Obviously."

He laughed at that, the warm, appreciative sound setting off little sparklers of pleasure along Evie's nerve endings. Maybe he really did like how apt she was to say whatever was on her mind.

"Don't sell yourself short, Evie. Rory might be the heart of Hillcrest House, but something tells me you're its soul."

Despite his recently acquired reputation as a jilted fiancé, Griffin was enjoying himself more than he likely should.

Something his father thought he did far too often.

He still didn't know why his father had taken such an interest in Hillcrest House. Though adorably quaint and comfortable, the Victorian hotel was hardly on par with the epic, ultramodern edifices the James brand boasted all over the world. New York, Chicago, San Francisco, Amsterdam, Dubai… Clearville? Even Griffin could figure out which one of those didn't belong.

Yet, for some reason, the boutique hotel remained on Frederick James's agenda.

But speaking of something—or *someone*—who didn't belong…

Despite the fact that she was sitting on a bar stool, Evie McClaren's posture was ramrod straight, her narrow nose and slightly pointed chin raised to a proud angle. But Griffin could see a slight flush rising in her high cheekbones, a hint of awareness in the sidelong glances she cast his way.

He leaned closer to be heard over the holiday tunes. Her perfume, something softly floral and feminine, such a contrast to her strictly business persona, intrigued him all the more and tempted him to linger.

With her blunt-cut dark hair, tall, slender body and serious personality, she was not his usual type. But his usual type—wealthy party girls—had started to bore him lately. To the point where he had proposed—sort of—to Alexa Mayhew. With his childhood friend pregnant as the result of a weekend fling, he'd thought a marriage based on friendship, affection and love could benefit them both.

But that was before Alexa reunited with the father of her unborn baby.

Griffin had willingly stepped aside, knowing Alexa loved Chance, but it did put him firmly back at square one when it came to the strings his father had attached to his trust fund. Strings that would strangle him if he didn't find a way to cut them, freeing him to finally go after his own dreams rather than living in the long shadows cast by the James empire.

"So, tell me, Ms. McClaren, what are you doing sitting in a bar alone on a Saturday night?"

Evie sighed, the exhale of air seeming to deflate her a little. But instead of answering his question, she asked one of her own. "Has there ever been something you wanted so badly you can picture it perfectly, and yet it's just out of reach?"

Griffin started, setting the martini back on the bar before he ended up spilling the drink. She might as well have read his mind and voiced the frustration building inside him. To the longing, the touch of desperation tinged with a hint of doubt that the dream would ever come true.

But Evie shook her head before giving him the chance to respond. "Of course not." Lifting her glass in a mocking toast, she said, "Look who I'm talking to."

"You'd be surprised," he told her, her words adding to a feeling of connection that had pulled at him from the moment he'd seen her sitting by herself.

Evie's blue eyes narrowed as she seemed to come to a conclusion. "Alexa's marrying another guy in a few days. Longing after a lost love just makes you…" She dismissed the emotion with a wave of her hand. Fortunately it was not the hand holding the martini or he might well have been down yet another shirt.

"Hopelessly romantic?" he filled in as her words trailed away.

"I was going more for *hopelessly pathetic*, but sure."

Griffin laughed. Evie was prickly on the outside, that was for sure, but he was from Southern California. A land of sun and sand. Of palm trees and cacti. But it was the lush, hardy bougainvillea Griffin pictured when he thought of Evie: tough yet beautiful, able to thrive despite heat and drought with its bright fuchsia blooms—and killer inch-long thorns.

If he tangled with the challenging brunette he'd likely end up with some scars to show for it. But he also knew the pleasure would be well worth the pain.

He wondered if she realized how that stubborn, defiant tilt to her head only managed to bring her lips ever closer. Wondered if she wasn't—subconsciously—asking to be kissed. Or maybe *he* was the one ready to beg to feel her lips beneath his own…

He cleared his throat and took another swallow of the bright red cocktail. "Enough about me. We were talking about you. What do you want, Evie?"

Tell me what you want, Evie, so I can do everything in my power to give it to you…

It was a ridiculous thought, especially for a man like Griffin. How many times had his father warned him about women who would chase after him for his family's wealth and prestige? As if he cared that they were as interested in his trust fund as they were his looks or his charm. As long as those women were focused on his wallet, Griffin didn't have to worry about guarding his heart.

He'd seen what loving a woman could do to a man. He'd seen what loving and losing his mother had done to his father. At fourteen, he'd witnessed how all the money and doctors and treatments in the world hadn't saved her from the agony of the cancer that spread through her body. Hadn't saved him from the pain of losing her.

So no, Griffin didn't care that those women were after his money. He made sure not to care too deeply about anything or anyone. And yet his breath caught in his chest as he waited to hear what Evie McClaren longed for.

"I want…" Her voice trailed off as her gaze met his, and Griffin felt his heart do some kind of strange slow-motion roll in his chest. Her elegant throat moved as she swallowed, and her dark lashes lowered in a languid blink.

The alcohol was catching up to her, but Griffin had no excuse for the riot of thoughts stumbling through his head like a drunk on a dance floor. *Me, Evie, you want me. But there's nothing hopeless about it because I am right here. Ready, willing and eager, and I am all yours.*

A laughing trio of girls bumped into them on their way to the bar, breaking the moment and allowing Griffin to suck in some much-needed air before he passed out dead on the floor. He reached for his glass even as Evie shook her head, as if she, too, was trying to snap out of whatever had held them spellbound.

Clearing her throat, she raised her chin and met his gaze head-on. "More than anything, I want Hillcrest House."

Griffin choked on the sugary-sweet sip of peppermint. "You—"

"I want to run my family's hotel."

He stared at her as what sounded like his father's rarely heard laughter echoed through his head. Evie's one great wish was for the very thing he longed to escape.

The towering James hotels stretched toward the heavens, but Griffin's dreams soared higher than that. From the time he was a teenager, he'd loved to fly. He loved the freedom, the excitement, the escape of leaving the earth behind to touch the skies. Of course, to hear his father tell it, Griffin had always had his head in the clouds, long before he'd gotten his pilot's license or his own plane. And Frederick James wanted nothing more than his only son's feet planted firmly on the ground and following in his own weighty footsteps.

But Evie's dreams hardly seemed like that much of a stretch. "You *are* running the hotel, right?"

"Temporarily," she pointed out. "While my aunt's been…away. She isn't sure she wants to run the hotel anymore. She's even…" Evie trailed off, but Griffin knew the words she didn't want to say.

Evelyn McClaren had been considering selling the hotel. That was the reason his father had sent Griffin to Hillcrest two months ago. He'd dug around a little, but at the time, Evie hadn't been talking.

Not the way she was now.

"I told her I would take on that role, managing the hotel full-time, and she could act as an advisor."

"That makes sense," he agreed. Far more sense than adding a quaint small-town Victorian property to the James brand.

"That's what I thought, too. Only my aunt isn't sure I'm the right person for the job."

Griffin could barely make out the words, but even without the loud music and laughter, he would have had a hard time hearing Evie as she made that admission. She ducked her head, the earlier confident tilt to her chin wilting as if she couldn't manage to hold his gaze. As if she were ashamed for somehow not being *enough*.

He'd spent years trying to convince his father he was

wise enough, mature enough, ready enough to take responsibility for the trust left to him by his maternal grandfather. Only to be shot down time and time again.

He knew the hollowed out, frustrated, helpless feeling, and it pissed him off for both of their sakes. "Your aunt's wrong, Evie. You know she's wrong."

A hint of color blossomed in her cheeks. "Yes, well, maybe you can convince her…" Her eyes widened as she quickly swallowed her words along with the rest of her martini, leaving Griffin dying to know exactly what Evie McClaren hadn't wanted to say.

Chapter Two

Chugging down a second martini when her head was already spinning from the first wasn't smart. But the temptation of alcohol was definitely the lesser of two evils when compared to the temptation of the man standing next to her.

His faith in her went to her head faster than any drink, and for a split second, she'd considered—what, exactly? Taking Griffin James home to her aunt to prove that she did have a life?

"Maybe I can convince her of what, Evie?"

"Nothing, it's ridiculous. The whole thing is ridiculous." Had she really spilled her guts, pouring out her hopes and dreams about running Hillcrest House to Griffin James, son of hotel magnate Frederick James? The man could have his pick of five-star hotels all over the world. Her dream of taking over the tiny Victorian must seem like such small potatoes in comparison. "You couldn't possibly understand what it's like not to have the chance to run your family hotel."

"I know what it's like not to have a choice."

Evie didn't know what to make of that statement, and before she could wrap her slightly foggy thoughts around its meaning, Griffin asked, "Did your aunt say why she doesn't think you are the right person for the job?"

"She's worried that I'll spend so much time focused on Hillcrest House that I'll forget to have a life of my own."

"Sounds like your aunt knows you pretty well."

"She always encouraged me to put my career first. For her to suddenly worry that I'm missing out on a man sweeping me off my feet makes no sense." Especially not considering the total disaster her one serious relationship ended up being. "I don't get it. It—doesn't add up."

Evie couldn't imagine what she'd said to make that sexy smirk appear on Griffin's lips. "Drives you crazy, doesn't it?"

Though Griffin phrased his words in a question, his confidence—and that smirk—said he knew her. But *that* was crazy. They were practically strangers, had spoken only a handful of times. He was the exact opposite of what Evie was looking for in a man. He was too cocky, too good-looking, too rich, too...*Griffin*.

And yet...no one would ever accuse him of not having a life. Raw energy all but pulsed from his pores, and standing so close to him, Evie felt, well, more *alive* than she had in...months? Years?

What do you want, Evie?

He'd asked the question like some kind of modern-day genie—or perhaps like a ridiculously sexy Santa—able to grant wishes with a single, seductive wink. And despite the answer she'd given, Hillcrest House hadn't been first and foremost on her mind as his deep voice washed over her.

Heaven help her, but a part of her she'd ignored, forgotten, over the past two years—the feminine, sensual part—had come alive in that moment. And it had taken every other logical, sensible, *sane* part of her not to answer his complicated question with one simple word.

You. I want you.

Just standing next to Griffin had a way of short-circuiting her brain. As if she had escaped from some kind of sensory deprivation chamber, her now starved body was soaking in everything. Or at least everything Griffin.

The flashing neon bar signs and Christmas lights combined with the loud music and scent of fried foods should have overwhelmed her. But it was the flash of Griffin's smile that blinded her. The deep rumble of his voice echoed in her ears. The scent of his expensive, woodsy cologne had her breathing deeper. And the thought of his kiss was more intoxicating than any one-hundred-proof liquor behind the bar.

He was driving her crazy, but Evie didn't do crazy. And she wasn't going to—

She jerked her attention away from Griffin to focus on the spindly gold-and-silver tree beside the register. "I have a plan," she blurted out, as much to remind herself as to answer Griffin. "One to prove to my aunt that I can run Hillcrest House and have a life."

Griffin made a disapproving sound. "Haven't you ever heard that life is what happens when you're busy making other plans?"

Evie frowned. "I've never understood that expression."

He chuckled at that. "Somehow I'm not surprised. But back to your life plan."

"All I have to do is show that there's more to me than my work. That I've scheduled time to spend with friends and family."

"You're penciling in your friends and family?"

"Who uses pencils anymore? I have them all programmed in here." Evie pulled her cell phone from the pocket of her skirt and then frowned at the numerous email alerts. Shoot, she'd forgotten she'd put her phone on Silent. She could have been spending the past half an hour responding... Only, judging by the way the letters seemed to dance on the too-bright screen, that might not be such a good idea.

"So what was tonight?"

"Tonight?"

"I don't see any friends or family around."

"Oh, tonight. Tonight was—" She sighed. "Tonight was date night." With her phone still in hand, she held up the screen for him to see. "Only he canceled."

"Seriously? Your date canceled in a text?"

Enough incredulity filled his voice that she couldn't help feeling a bit defensive. "It wasn't Wade's fault. He had an emergency at work. I told him I understood."

She had, after all, canceled on him. Twice. Although she'd at least done so with a phone call.

"Because work comes first."

"Exactly." Evie cringed. Crap, that wasn't what she was supposed to say. If she was going to prove to her aunt that she had something more in her life than her job, she needed to be a lot more convincing.

"Evie, Evie." Griffin shook his head in disappointment. "All work and no play..."

"Makes me dull, I know."

She didn't know why that admission would make his sexy grin widen even further. "Not dull, Evie." He leaned closer as he spoke, the warmth of his breath against her ear setting off tiny shock waves inside her. "Never dull."

Though she could hear him perfectly, she leaned closer as if some of that easy confidence radiating from him might somehow rub off on her. His eyes gleamed despite the dim lighting, and she could almost believe she saw her image shimmering there. Or not her own image, but Griffin's image of her. Someone smart, sexy… Someone…fun.

"In fact, I was thinking to myself how…sharp you are. Sharp enough to know working hard isn't going to get you what you wish for."

Evie swallowed at the phrase.

"But playing hard will?" And why had that come out sounding as if she was seriously considering the possibility instead of completely dismissing it?

"It's like you said. Your aunt doesn't think you can run Hillcrest House and have a life. All you have to do is prove her wrong."

She swallowed the laughter bubbling up inside her. Right, because what Santa worth his sleigh granted only a single wish? *Hillcrest and a life and still one more wish to go…*

Griffin leaned back on the bar stool, staring with disinterest at a replay of a recent college bowl game as he waited for Evie to return. He frowned as he glanced at the narrow hallway that led to the restrooms. He'd spooked her earlier. Had he needed further proof that he'd pushed her too hard, it was sitting on the bar next to him in the form of her cell phone. He couldn't imagine that she went anywhere without the tether to her job.

Unable to resist, Griffin swiped a thumb across the screen. He wasn't surprised to see a photo of Hillcrest

House as the screensaver. The towering Victorian was a gorgeous property. He'd give his father that.

But it wasn't the lacy trim, carved columns or elegant turrets reaching toward a clear blue sky that had the breath stalling in Griffin's throat. Instead, it was the image of Evie standing on the front steps. She was dressed more casually than he had seen her before, in a yellow-and-white-checked sundress that made her look young and—Griffin grinned, knowing what she'd likely think of the description—sweet. A small smile teased her lips, but the tiny tell gave away the pleasure and pride she took in calling the hotel home. Running it was more than a job to her.

So much more than a job that she was willing to date some loser to make a point to her aunt. Griffin scowled at the phone before sliding it into his pocket. What kind of idiot would stand up a woman as intriguing as Evie McClaren? She'd accepted Workaholic Wade's blow-off excuse too easily. Because her job came first for her, as she said?

Or because some other loser had made her believe she deserved to come in second?

A hand clapped down on his shoulder, distracting Griffin from the troubling thought. The blond man who'd egged him into placing a friendly wager on the game of pool hopped onto Evie's abandoned bar stool. "Hey, man, good game."

"Just my lucky night, I guess." Or so he hoped...

"Billy Cummings." After introducing himself, the man glanced at Griffin's candy-cane martini with a look of disgust. "I feel like I should at least buy you a real drink."

"I already won the bet. You don't owe me."

"Yeah, well..." Billy paused, tipping his bottle of beer

back. "The thing is, I probably should have warned you what a competitive SOB Travis is."

Griffin chuckled at that. "Maybe next time I'll let him win."

Billy sputtered before wiping his mouth. "You sure about that?"

Griffin shrugged. He had a competitive streak of his own, but he'd never been a sore loser. "Yeah. Why?"

"Because I think Travis has already set his eye on the next prize."

Griffin turned, following the direction of the beer bottle Billy used to point to a spot behind him. And every thought he'd ever had about playing fair, following the rules or losing gracefully flew out the window the second he saw Travis spinning Evie McClaren across the dance floor.

He swore beneath his breath, but before he could charge through the crowd, Billy caught his biceps. At the glare Griffin shot him, Billy raised both arms in an "innocent man" gesture. "Hey, don't kill the messenger! But as the son of the town sheriff, I should warn you that my dad has a funny sense of justice. Get in a fight and he'll throw you and Travis into the same cell to 'work things out.'"

Watching as Travis's hand moved down Evie's hip, Griffin thought cage fighting might be in order for the night. "And?" he gritted out.

"And if both you and Travis are locked up... Well, then, I guess I'll be the one taking Evie McClaren home. So you might wanna think this through."

Griffin exhaled, as if trying to cool the jealous rage burning inside him. "So I can't hit him," he stated with certainty. "Not even once?"

Billy grinned. "That's up to you, man."

As Griffin pushed his way toward the dance floor, he reminded himself that he wasn't the jealous type. He never got close enough to a woman to care that much.

But right now, Travis was the one close enough. Close enough to murmur something in Evie's ear. Close enough to wrap an arm around her slender waist. Close enough to feel her body pressed to his…

And Griffin cared. He cared too damn much.

But the moment he met Evie's eyes over the other man's shoulder, Griffin's tensed muscles relaxed. Travis didn't know it, and Evie might not even realize it, but Griffin had already won. His victory was written in the awareness of her midnight blue eyes, the slight parting of her lips, in the subtle but stubborn lift to her chin.

Evie didn't need someone to fight for her. She'd pick her own battles, as she had with her goal to prove herself to her aunt, and she would do so on her own terms.

Her own terms were completely ridiculous, of course. Dates made online and confirmed—or canceled—by text like some kind of tax audit. She deserved much more than that, and now he was going to be the one to prove it to her.

Because with that telling glance, she'd picked him.

Travis glared at Griffin's interruption, looking like he was ready to line up another shot. Only this time, he wasn't planning on using a cue ball. "Back off, James. The lady and I are…busy."

Although he recognized a goad when he heard one, Griffin didn't take the bait. Ignoring the other man, he kept his focus on Evie. He could see the effect of the two martinis as she swayed toward him slightly.

Or maybe he could hope that something more powerful than alcohol was involved. Like the attraction that had drawn him out to the dance floor. Like the attraction that had drawn him to her the first time they met.

Even in the neon glare from the beer signs and the flickering holiday lights hanging around the place, Evie's skin had a pale glow that reminded him of moonlight. Her dark hair was straight as straw and yet soft as silk. Another fascinating contrast in a fascinating woman. She was tough and yet vulnerable. Razor sharp and yet surprisingly unsure.

Maybe he was more like his father than he wanted to admit, but Griffin knew how to spot a weakness and how to exploit it to get what he wanted. And what he wanted more than anything was Evie in his arms.

"I thought about what we talked about earlier, and I've come up with a proposition for you," he said to Evie. Her eyebrows rose at that and he swore beneath his breath at the slip of the tongue. "A business proposition."

Travis snorted. "Who wants to talk business on a Saturday night?"

Griffin didn't bother hiding his smile as Evie eased away from the other man. "What kind of…proposition?" she asked, and all the blood pounding in his veins shot straight south.

He'd left the *business* out of his proposition by accident. Why did he feel like Evie's omission was on purpose? And he couldn't help thinking that maybe the only weakness being exploited here…was his.

Still, he held out his hand. "Dance with me, and I'll tell you all about it."

Barely glancing back at her previous partner, Evie said, "Thank you for the dance, Travis. This next one is, um—"

"Mine," Griffin confirmed, reaching out to entwine her delicate fingers with his own. "All mine."

Travis swore beneath his breath, a two-time loser in the evening, but Griffin paid no attention as the man stalked off the dance floor. Victory had never been so sweet as Evie twined her slender arms around his neck. Her breath was soft and peppermint scented against his lips as she asked, "So, what is this offer?"

"Me."

Her dark eyebrows gathered in an adorable frown as she tried to work out what he was saying. "Yes," she agreed, before stating, "your offer. What is it?"

"No, sweetheart, you don't understand. I'm offering you my…services."

Evie's jaw dropped, and it took all the strength he had not to erase the distance between them and press a kiss against her parted pink lips. He contented himself with pulling her close enough to feel the softness of her breasts against his chest and the brush of her thigh between his own.

"I'm offering to help you find a balance between your professional and personal lives." He congratulated himself on a phrasing that would appeal to Evie's logical mind.

"So we'd… What, exactly? Pretend to go out to fool my aunt into thinking I have a life?"

He couldn't help it. He laughed. "Or we could simply go out together with no subterfuge involved. Take tonight, for example—hanging out at a bar, having a few drinks, dancing… This is what having a life feels like, Evie."

And yet for all the *living* he'd done during his teens and twenties, he'd never felt anything quite like holding Evie McClaren in his arms. He couldn't remember a time when his pulse had soared so high outside a cockpit.

She shook her head as she swallowed and focused over his shoulder. "I'm not much for playing games."

"This isn't a game, Evie. It's a dance."

"I'm not sure there's a difference."

A hint of vulnerability eased through a tiny crack in her brash exterior, and just like that, he knew. This was a woman who could slip through *his* defenses. If one of them should have been running... Hell, he should have hit the door at full speed the second she placed her hand in his. Instead, he moved closer and gave that same hand a squeeze.

"Of course there is. In a dance, I lead and you follow."

"And in a game?"

"In any game the two of us play, I would follow wherever you lead."

Had someone asked Evie how far she'd be willing to go to keep Hillcrest House, she would have said she'd do anything. But never in her wildest dreams would she have expected dating Griffin James to somehow fall into that category.

Not that she'd agreed to his plan. At least, not yet.

And how had she'd gone from sitting alone after being stood up to suddenly having her choice of men on the dance floor? She didn't exactly remember saying yes to Travis Parker, but she couldn't recall saying no, either. Once she found herself in his arms, she'd hoped to enjoy herself.

But even though it had been Travis in her arms, it was Griffin on her mind.

Travis was handsome enough, but for all his lady-killer charm, she might as well have been dancing with—well, Wade the accountant, a man she'd chosen for his distinct lack of charm.

No, she couldn't blame alcohol or abstinence or anyone other than Griffin James for the pulse pounding in her veins and the heat pooling in her belly. And now he was offering—

"I need to go," she said as the music ended, startled to realize it wasn't the same song that had been playing when Griffin first stepped onto the dance floor. One had blended into another—and then another?—as they swayed together.

Oh, this wasn't good. None of this was good.

Especially not the way he trailed his hand down her arm and linked his fingers with hers. "I'll take you home."

Jerking her hand from his, she pointed out, "It wasn't an invitation."

Anticipating some kind of teasing comment, he surprised her by insisting, "You've been drinking, Evie. I'm not letting you drive."

Not letting her? Everything in her should have rebelled at the arrogant comment. Only the demand didn't sound controlling so much as it did caring...

But it wasn't her nature to give in easily. "Maybe I'll ask Travis to take me home."

"Evie." The sound of his voice sent shivers down her spine. "You don't want Travis."

And there it was again. That question hanging in the charged air between them.

What do you want?

And this time, there was no silencing the answer that came to mind. "I want you."

Chapter Three

Evie awoke with a low groan. Sunlight pierced through her eyelids and straight to her brain. She longed to reach down and pull the covers up over her head, but that would require moving. And moving at the moment seemed... unwise.

She never should have had that second peppermint martini after Griffin—

Oh, God. Griffin.

Evie didn't know if it was her heart or her stomach that gave the sudden, sickening lurch. Fuzzy bits and pieces of the night before pounded away at her temples. Her date canceling... Griffin showing up...his offer... And finally, her desperate, humiliating response...

I want you.

Could a person actually die of embarrassment? Because that admission right there might have been the nail in her coffin.

What had she been thinking? And more important, what had she *done*?

Still unwilling to open her eyes, Evie swallowed, shuddering a bit, and slid her hand slowly across the smooth sheets.

For her first several months in Clearville, she had stayed at the hotel. But in an effort to separate her personal life from her professional one, Evie had moved into a small cottage on the grounds. And thank God she had. How mortifying would it have been for a guest—or worse, an employee—to see Griffin James guiding her down the floral-patterned hallway and into one of the rooms!

Instead, Griffin had driven her to the cottage. The December night had been cool and crisp, a hint of woodsmoke from a distant chimney mixing with the ocean scent in the air. She'd stopped to look up at the stars, so much brighter in Clearville than they had seemed back in Portland. Or maybe she had never paused long enough to notice the way she had last night.

"Beautiful," Griffin had murmured.

But he hadn't been looking up at the night sky. He'd been staring down at her. He'd brushed her hair back from her face, his hands warm against her chilled skin. The sweet rush of desire weakened her knees, and Evie had swayed toward him, certain he was going to kiss her and then—

And then…

And then…nothing. Like waking from a dream just as it was getting to the good part, Evie had no idea what had happened next. Had Griffin kissed her? Had she kissed him? Had she done *more* than kiss him?

Her hand moved across the bed, and Evie held her breath, dreading the moment when her palm went from discovering cool, soft cotton to warm, masculine skin. But her fingers inched along, encountering nothing more shocking than a ruffled lace pillow.

Evie forced her eyelids open and cringed at the sun peeking through the curtains. Wait. *Sun?* She shot into a sitting position, groaning again at the way her head and stomach joined together in a nauseating mutiny. She had a split second of relief at seeing the other side of the bed empty. The sheets were still tucked in along the far edge of the mattress, the pillow right in place. No sign that Griffin had slept—or done anything else—there.

But she barely took time to exhale before she threw back the covers and glanced at the nightstand where she always charged her phone. The device wasn't there. Which was why she hadn't heard the alarm go off. Which was why she had no idea what time it was.

Crap! Evie scrambled out of bed. She was supposed to be helping Rory and their aunt decorate one of Hillcrest's banquet rooms for Alexa's bridal shower that morning.

What was her aunt going to think? Forget the fact that Evie was one of the bridesmaids and Alexa was soon to be part of the family. What did it say for her work ethic to no-show a hotel event?

Evie noticed the clock on the dresser and released a huge breath. Eight thirty. Later than she'd slept in years, but plenty of time before Alexa's shower at ten. Still, she needed to hurry. Yanking open the closet, she reached for the first hanger she found. Her aunt and Rory would be showing up soon. They'd stored some of the presents at the cottage and—

The thought had barely crossed her mind when the sound of female voices coming from the front of the house reached Evie. She clutched the hastily grabbed clothes to her chest, but a knock on the front door warned her it was too late.

She hated being caught unprepared. What had she been thinking last night? She had to have lost her mind. Drinking, dancing…actually considering taking Griffin up on his ridiculous plan?

After the shower, she would call and thank him for seeing her home. She'd swallow her embarrassment long enough to tell him she was grateful that he hadn't taken advantage of her foolish behavior and then flat-out refuse his ridiculous offer to fake date her.

The knocking started again, followed by Rory's voice. "Evie? Are you in there? I tried calling your cell…"

Great. Just great! This was why she didn't date! She was no good at juggling so many things at once. She didn't have time to—

Have a life? Griffin's mocking voice sounded in her mind, as sexily as if he'd whispered the words in her ear. *Working hard isn't going to get you what you wish for.*

Ignoring the shivers of desire racing across her goose-fleshed skin, Evie tossed the clothes onto the bed. She rubbed her hands over her face and pushed her hair back behind her ears. It was time to face the music before her cousin called out the National Guard.

After taking a deep breath, she opened the front door to her wide-awake and perfectly put-together aunt and cousin. "Hi, um, sorry, I'm not dressed yet." Feeling more out of sorts by the second, she confessed, "I sort of slept in this morning."

The two women exchanged a look as they stepped inside the small, shabby chic living room. "You never sleep in," Rory stated. "Are you feeling okay?"

"Fine. I'm just…" *Hungover? Humiliated?* Ignoring the shots her conscience was taking at her, she weakly finished, "I'm fine. If you can give me fifteen minutes or so, I'll help with the presents."

"Wait." Rory's brows drew together as she called a halt to Evie's quick escape. "Didn't you have a date last night with your mystery man?"

Evie had never meant to make her date sound the least bit mysterious. She hadn't given any details because she hadn't wanted to admit she'd canceled twice. Leave it to Rory to spin some romantic fantasy in her mind about Wade.

Right. Because that was ridiculous. Unlike the romantic fantasies about Griffin James spinning through Evie's head! She swore she could almost smell his aftershave mixed in with the scent of brewing coffee and could only hope that was some hangover-induced hallucination and—

Wait. She took another deep breath, making sure she wasn't imagining things. But no, she could practically taste the strong dark roast calling her name.

"Right, Evie? Evie?"

Frowning, she turned her attention from the kitchen behind her and back to her aunt and cousin. "Sorry, what were you saying?"

"Well, I was trying to tell Aunt E about this guy you've been seeing, but you've been keeping all the juicy details to yourself, haven't you?"

"Right. That's right." Had she set the timer on the pot the night before? She didn't think so, but she must have. "About last night…" Evie began, ready to tell the truth about her nondate with Wade. The truth about the rest of the night would follow her to her grave.

But before she could explain, a faint sound interrupted. A slight squeak and then the familiar and yet entirely out-of-place sound of water running.

"Is that—" Rory frowned "—the shower?"

This wasn't happening. This couldn't possibly be happening. "I, um, you know how old this cottage is. The pipes are always rattling."

"Rattling, sure, but I don't remember the tap turning on by itself."

"Evelyn Marie McClaren." Evie cringed as her aunt interrupted the inane conversation about rusty taps. "Is there someone here?"

Rory's jaw dropped. "Oh, my gosh! Did your date spend the night?"

"No!" Oh, no. No, no, no! This couldn't be happening!

But if the sound of running water was unmistakable, so, too, was the opening of the bathroom door and the masculine voice that drifted down the hall. "Hey, babe, I thought you were going to join me."

And now it was official. She'd learned without a doubt that dying of embarrassment was not possible.

Unfortunately.

Griffin had been discovered in some rather compromising situations over the years, but he'd never deliberately set out to get caught. Until he stepped into Evie McClaren's living room wearing nothing but a towel.

He'd known during the drive to the tiny cottage the night before that he'd be putting Evie to bed rather than taking her there. She had nearly fallen asleep on the way home and had been swaying on her feet as she'd stared up at the night sky.

"Wishing on a star?" he'd asked.

"I don't believe in wishes."

But he had heard enough longing in her voice to know she still made them even if she had given up on them coming true.

Not this time, Griffin had vowed. Not if he had anything to say about it.

And as it turned out, he did. Unable to leave Evie on her own even after she'd crawled into bed—alone—he'd spent an uncomfortable night on the cramped love seat. He'd started a pot of coffee and was in the bathroom, contemplating shaving with a bright pink razor he'd found in the medicine cabinet, when he'd heard feminine voices.

Sound carried in the small cottage, and he'd known this was his chance.

"Sorry to interrupt," he said with a smile at the three McClaren women. "I didn't realize Evie had company."

"I think that should be our line," the older woman murmured.

"You must be Evie's aunt," he said, holding out his hand as if he'd stepped out of a boardroom wearing a suit rather than out of the bathroom wearing a towel. "She's told me so much about you."

From what he'd learned of the serious, driven businesswoman, he'd expected, well, an older version of Evie. But this woman was far more at ease and amused than her niece. Faint lines crinkled around her eyes as she tried to hide a smile. "I'm afraid I can't say the same. It seems our Evie has been keeping secrets."

"You can say that again," Rory muttered, a distrusting scowl on her pretty face.

"Ms. McClaren, nice to see you again."

Evie's cousin offered a sound that made it clear she'd seen more than enough of him. Griffin supposed he couldn't blame her, considering the last time he'd just punched her brother, Chance, in the face.

As for Evie... Glancing at her now, he had to swallow a chuckle. Her hair was slightly mussed, and a pillow crease lined one soft cheek. Wearing a long-sleeved bubble gum–

pink top over a pair of checked flannel pajama bottoms and not a speck of makeup, she looked young…and vulnerable. A word he never would have associated with the woman he'd met two months ago. Her dark blue eyes were huge in her pale face, and those same protective instincts from the night before rose up inside him again.

"I know this must all seem sudden," he said, "but from the moment Evie and I met, I haven't been able to get her off my mind. I've been counting the days until I could come back here and be the man to sweep her off her feet."

"Have you lost your mind along with your c-clothes?" Evie demanded a few minutes later.

She tried to glare at Griffin. She really did. But every time she glanced his way, her glare turned into more of a stare as she took in the broad shoulders, muscular arms and abs that put a six-pack to shame. Not to mention the towel. A floral-printed, pastel *hand towel* that he had wrapped around that lean waist.

Unconcerned that he was a loosened terry-cloth knot away from naked, Griffin shrugged. "I was following along with your plan."

"My plan? Griffin, I might not remember everything that happened last night, but I can guarantee you that no amount of candy-cane martinis would have led me to a plan that included introducing you to my aunt while you were wearing a towel!"

"Evie… I'm…hurt. Really. You don't remember anything about last night?" A husky tease entered his voice. The towel parted slightly as he stepped closer, revealing a muscular thigh that led down to well-defined calves covered with a light dusting of dark blond hair.

Reaching out, he pushed a strand of hair away from her cheek, reminding her with a painful sense of awareness that she likely had a serious case of bedhead. She had to look a hot mess while Griffin was inches away, looking…hot.

"I didn't say that I don't remember anything. Just that I don't remember everything." But standing so close to him, bits and pieces of the night before were coming back to her. Something about wishes and stars and sweet dreams as Griffin had—oh, good grief! Had he actually tucked her in?

Heat filled Evie's cheeks and she honestly wished the night was nothing more than a blank slate. "But I'm not talking about last night. I'm talking about this morning and how you—"

She waved a hand at his nearly naked state and then gasped as he caught her wrist and pressed her palm right against that warm, bare chest. His heart beat in a strong, steady rhythm while her own pulse skyrocketed out of the stratosphere.

"Evie," he said patiently. "Did you see the look on your aunt's face?"

She had. After the initial wide-eyed surprise had worn off, her aunt had looked…pleased. Happy, even.

"Your brilliant plan is working." Griffin gave her wrist a gentle squeeze before letting go. "Unless you'd rather have me go to your aunt and cousin, and tell them that this morning was a joke and you and I aren't romantically involved."

Was that what she wanted? To be back at square one with little chance of proving herself to her aunt? "No, no. Don't do that," she argued, belatedly realizing she still had her hand pressed to his chest even without Griffin holding it there and she felt that wild rush again. Only this time, it wasn't her heart pounding like mad but Griffin's, pulsing beneath her palm.

Evie snatched her arm back, resisting the urge to rub her hand against the material of her pajamas to erase the burning imprint of his skin. "I mean, they've already jumped to their own conclusions. What would it hurt to keep up the ruse? Just until my aunt sees that I'm the perfect person to run Hillcrest House."

"Evie..."

Picking up on the patronizing tone in his voice, she felt her shoulders stiffen. "What?" she asked defensively. She was well aware that a man like Griffin James—who would never have to pretend to have a life—couldn't possibly understand why faking it was the best she could do. "It's a good plan. Brilliant, if you didn't say so yourself. Are you backing out already?"

"Not a chance."

She shouldn't have felt so relieved by his promise. A means to an end, she reminded herself. As long as Griffin was willing to play his part, she didn't have to try to find someone else to fill the role.

"I need to get ready. I'm supposed to be helping Rory and Aunt E decorate." As more and more of their conversation from the night before drifted back, Evie held up a warning finger. "And don't even think about crashing Alexa's shower."

But Griffin only grinned at her warning. "What about *your* shower, Evie?" he asked. "Any chance of me crashing that?"

Chapter Four

Half an hour later, Evie rushed into Hillcrest's parlor. She hated being late, and she'd had an added incentive for taking the fastest shower on record. She wasn't sure if more than a dozen water droplets had hit her body. But the thought of Griffin joining her had had Evie rushing through at warp speed.

Not because she honestly thought he would invade her privacy, but because of the unrelenting, undeniable, unwanted way he'd invaded her thoughts. She hadn't been able to strip away an article of clothing without imagining him watching her. Helping her.

Sometime during her five-second shower, however, Griffin had left the cottage. She'd found a note beneath her phone on the tiny kitchen table, telling her he'd be back after the shower—bridal shower, he'd felt the need to point out—to pick her up and take her to her car.

And at that, Evie had thought her humiliation complete.

She hadn't given a thought to her phone—or her car—since the night before.

"Sorry I'm late," she said to her aunt and cousin as she stepped into the parlor. The warm cherry wainscot, pale pink walls and floral-print sofas were the perfect combination of elegance and romance. Extra seating had been brought in for the bridal shower, along with two tables—one for presents and another for finger foods, punch and cake—and both spreads were decorated with the blue and silver colors of the winter wedding.

"I think we'll forgive you this time," Aunt Evelyn said, "considering…"

Evie's cheeks heated as her aunt's voice trailed away. She really didn't want her aunt considering anything about what she and Griffin James hadn't done the night before.

This was all a mistake, a misunderstanding, a make-believe relationship. Three M-words instead of the 4-F plan that had started this in the first place.

But if she admitted that, she would *be* right back in the first place, back at square one, with the wedding days away and no date in sight. "I know this whole…thing has come as a surprise, but I promise you, my…relationship won't interfere with work."

"Why on earth not? If I had a man like that in my bed, you wouldn't see me for a week."

"Aunt E!" Evie protested, the shock missing from her aunt's voice this morning clearly present in her own.

"What?" her aunt questioned. "Granted, I'm old enough to be his mother, but I'm not dead yet." And with that announcement, her aunt excused herself to go raid the hotel's wine cellar for some champagne and apple cider for the bride-to-be.

Shaking her head as her aunt left the room, Evie murmured, "Honestly, I don't know what has gotten into her."

"What's gotten into *her*?" Rory echoed. "How about what's gotten into you?"

"Look, I know this must all seem...sudden." Evie cringed a little as she glanced around the room at the festive clusters of blue and silver balloons tied to the backs of the chairs, the banner draped behind the tables spelling out Alexa's and Chance's names... A banner that a few months ago would have linked Alexa and *Griffin*.

Rory made a strangled sound. "What were you thinking?"

"I was thinking that I deserve a life of my own. That I want to go out and go dancing with a man who's fun and exciting and interested in me!"

And even though Evie wanted to believe she was simply following the plan, playing her part, every word she'd said was true. She wanted all of that and more...

"And you really think it's all a coincidence?" Rory was asking as Evie tried to bring her thoughts back from Griffin to focus on the ultimate goal.

What do you want, Evie?

Hillcrest House. She wanted Hillcrest House. And—heaven help her—she wanted Griffin James.

"At a time when Aunt E is considering selling the hotel, Griffin James just happens to show up here?"

"He's here for the wedding. You know he and Alexa grew up together. Other than her grandmother, Griffin is the closest thing Alexa has to family. That's why she asked him to walk her down the aisle."

"Sure, now," Rory pointed out. "But what about two months ago? What brought him here then?"

Evie opened her mouth, but no words came out.

No. It wouldn't be. It *couldn't* be. Evie had done her

homework before stepping in for her aunt. She'd researched what made five-star hotels five-star, and almost every article she'd read mentioned Frederick James and his chain of exclusive hotels.

How many times had she come across a James hotel in articles and advertisements? The brand's logo was a magical creature with the body, tail and legs of a lion and the head and wings of an eagle. A creature known as a gryphon.

Or…griffin.

She'd seen the emblem lording over the James hotels—towering steel and chrome and glass edifices. Soaring above the skylines in New York, Chicago, San Francisco, Amsterdam. State-of-the-art, ultramodern buildings that won global recognition for their cutting-edge designs.

Everything Hillcrest House was not.

Hillcrest was quaint. It was old-fashioned. The aging structure held fast to its history, clinging with a sense of nostalgia to a more romantic time.

The idea of Hillcrest House boasting the James symbol seemed as likely as a luxury car manufacturer slapping its logo on a horse-drawn carriage and rolling it out as an upcoming model. Nothing about it added up, and Evie grasped the logical conclusion like a lifeline.

"You're wrong about Griffin," Evie insisted.

Doubt filled Rory's expression as she said, "I hope so, Evie. For both our sakes, I really do."

"So, how did the two of you meet?"

"Was it love at first sight?"

"What are your plans for after the wedding?"

The questions were nothing unusual for a bridal shower, only none of the curious women were looking at Alexa. All eyes had turned to Evie.

"It wasn't me," Rory protested when Evie shot her a look. "I didn't say a word."

"Are you kidding?" Debbie Pirelli, owner of Sugar & Spice Café and the exclusive designer of Hillcrest House's wedding cakes, exclaimed. "News of you dirty dancing with Griffin James is all over town!"

Laughter and whistles followed that pronouncement, and Evie's face burned even as she tried to remind herself that these women were Rory and Alexa's friends. That they were teasing her and not making fun of her. But she'd learned her lesson with Eric Laughlin. Two and a half years ago, she'd told everyone who would listen about her "perfect" boyfriend. He'd fooled her completely and Evie had fallen for every stupid, sappy line. She'd sworn she would never make a fool of herself over a man again.

Keeping that vow had been easy. She'd buried most of her emotions right alongside her broken heart. Yet somehow here she was, once again, with her private life open for discussion, building herself up for an epic fail. Her cousin's words played against her own doubts, and Evie's thoughts had been ping-ponging back and forth throughout the entire shower.

Rory was wrong about Griffin.

What if she was wrong about Griffin?

Griffin was interested in her.

What if Griffin's only interest was in the hotel?

At least Debbie had waited until the end of the event to start her interrogation. Only Alexa and her bridesmaids were still seated around the table amid empty dessert plates sprinkled with devil's food cake crumbs, a rainbow of discarded ribbons and bows, and colorful wads of wrapping paper. But with all the attention focused on her,

Evie felt as though the few bites of rich, decadent choco-late cake she'd eaten earlier were lodged in her throat.

Without waiting for Evie to respond, Debbie turned to Alexa. "You must have known about this, right?"

The beautiful blonde shook her head as she fingered the ribbons on a "bouquet" made up of the brightly col-ored bows pulled from her presents. Even at five months pregnant, Alexa possessed a grace and elegance Evie envied. Raised to be the face of the philanthropic orga-nization started by Virginia Mayhew, her wealthy grand-mother, Alexa was always perfectly poised.

"I've been so busy with wedding details I haven't had a chance to spend much time with Griffin." Glancing be-tween the two cousins, Alexa said, "I know this whole sit-uation is unusual. Having Griffin give me away when—"

"You almost married him?" Evie blurted out the words without thinking and winced when Rory's shoe con-nected with her shin beneath the table.

Alexa shook her head. "We wouldn't have gone through with it. When I first found out I was pregnant, I was...overwhelmed. Chance was half a world away and not a man who had any interest in being a husband or father. Or at least that's what I thought, and Griffin..." She laughed. "Well, he has a habit of rescuing damsels in distress. He's been looking out for me since we were eight years old."

All women not named McClaren offered a heartfelt *awww* at Griffin the hero.

"It was never anything more than friendship between us. He thought maybe if we married..."

"If you married, what?" That eager question had come from Sophia Pirelli Cameron, Debbie's sister-in-law, sav-ing Evie's shin from another kick had she been the one to insist Alexa continue.

"Griffin's grandfather left him an inheritance, but the terms of the trust are ambiguous, to say the least. Griffin's been working like a madman to try to prove himself to his father. He thought us getting married might convince his father that he's settled and responsible enough to pursue his own dreams."

A handful of words shouldn't have had the power to turn Evie's world upside down, but everything she knew—everything she *thought* she knew—about Griffin was suddenly in doubt. Flirtatious lady's man Griffin sacrificing his freedom as a bachelor to marry a woman carrying another man's child? Golden boy, heir-to-the-empire Griffin struggling to prove his worth to his father? Live-for-the-moment Griffin longing after some distant dream?

"But wasn't Griffin the one who encouraged you to tell Chance that you were pregnant with his child?" Lindsay Kincaid, another of Alexa's bridesmaids, leaned forward in her chair, engrossed in the story.

Alexa nodded. "He did. But that's the kind of man Griffin is. He'd never put his own happiness ahead of someone he cared about."

The women gave another group sigh, but Rory muttered beneath her breath, "Or maybe he found another way to impress his father."

"Right." Evie didn't bother to keep her own voice down. "Because it's not like any man would actually be interested in me for me." Even though a wealth of sarcasm weighted her words, she had to wonder. Really, what was more likely—Griffin wanting to pretend to be her boyfriend to make her dreams come true or trying to find a way to cash in on his own?

"All right," Debbie demanded. "What is going on between the two of you this morning?"

Not one to beat around the bush, Evie blurted out, "Our aunt is thinking of selling the hotel."

"Sell Hillcrest House?"

As the bridesmaids voiced their protests to the idea of the historic Clearville landmark being sold, Evie's stomach rolled at the hint of guilt that touched Alexa's lovely face.

"That is the reason why Griffin and I came to Clearville in the first place," Alexa confessed. "His father heard the hotel might be for sale, but Griffin has spent the past two months overseeing a construction site overseas and he hasn't mentioned Hillcrest House since."

A sheen of tears filled her eyes as she added, "I don't have nearly the claim that you do, but the hotel is special to me, too. Chance and I couldn't imagine having our wedding anywhere else."

"Did your aunt tell you why she's thinking of selling?" Lindsay asked.

Because she doesn't trust me to run it. Evie had failed her aunt before. If Rory was right and the James empire was ready to throw its impressive gold-plated global hat in the ring, what chance did Evie have of changing her aunt's mind?

With James hotels spanning the world and technology being what it was, Griffin could work 24/7 from almost anywhere. After ordering a mouthwatering breakfast of fluffy scrambled eggs, crisp toast and perfectly cooked apple-smoked bacon, he had spent the next several hours in his suite, making phone calls, returning emails, going over the latest progress reports for a new hotel. But in the back of his mind, he'd known he was killing time until he could see Evie again and before long, he'd made his way down to the lobby.

The last time he'd been at Hillcrest House, the welcoming area had been decked out for fall. Now the dark walnut panels were trimmed with all the holiday colors as green garlands dotted with bright bursts of holly circled the carved square columns and enormous red-and-gold wreaths hung on the walls. Lit trees glowed from every corner, and even the coffee table in front of him held a small wooden sleigh filled with pine cones and silver bells.

All of the decorations that were conspicuously missing from Evie's place.

Perhaps being surrounded by so much holiday cheer, she hadn't felt the need to decorate the tiny cottage. Griffin doubted that was the reason. He had the feeling Evie was seriously missing the Christmas spirit, while he seemed to have suddenly found his.

He'd even asked the age-old question.

What do you want, Evie?

Griffin knew all he wanted was to make her wishes come true.

He tossed the flyer of upcoming holiday events he'd been flipping through onto the table and stood as he caught sight of her. She'd traded in her long-sleeved shirt and flannel pj's from that morning for an emerald green silk shirt tucked into a straight black skirt. A pair of shiny calf-skimming boots made her legs look endless and sexy as hell.

His pulse hit full throttle as her determined stride carried her across the lobby. She faltered for a split second as she caught sight of him, but she recovered quickly as she headed straight toward him.

"Hey, sweetheart, how was the shower?"

She scowled at the wink he shot her but didn't say a word as she caught his arm and practically dragged him across the floral-patterned carpet and toward the double doors leading to the front porch.

Midmorning fog wrapped the house, and the air was cool and damp. Low-lying clouds hovered above the tree line, but that was nothing compared to the storm gathering in Evie's expression.

"As flattered as I am by how eager you are to get me alone, why do I get the feeling something's wrong?"

Dropping her hold on his arm, Evie walked to the garland-wrapped railing before turning back. She stood with her arms crossed over her chest in the same spot where he and her cousin Chance had had their fight during his first visit.

No doubt about it. If he ended up with any blood on his shirt this time, it would be courtesy of Evie McClaren. "As if you don't know."

"Oh, come on! The shower couldn't have been that bad."

Unless she'd told everyone that his spending the night wasn't how it had appeared. His amped-up anticipation deflated, leaving him strangely disappointed. After she'd gutted her way through the introductions to her aunt and cousin, he'd really thought Evie was going to go along with the plan.

Taking up her aunt's challenge, but on her own terms, was so…Evie. He didn't like thinking of her backing down. Or maybe it was more than that. Maybe he wasn't ready to let go of any plan that had the two of them spending more time together.

"Everyone knows we left the bar together last night."

"Small-town gossip, but doesn't that work perfectly with your plan?"

"My plan? Was this ever really my plan, Griffin, or was this your plan from the very start?"

"You're gonna have to help me out a little here. I'm guessing the sofa in your living room isn't nearly as comfortable as your bed—and by the way, you have to at least give me a little credit for choosing to sleep there instead of with you where I wanted to be." Another choked sound escaped her throat. "So can you cut me a little slack and tell me what you're talking about?"

"I'm talking about why you're really here."

"For Alexa and Chance's wedding. You know that."

"And that's the only reason? It's not because, say, you heard my aunt is thinking about selling the hotel?"

Griffin hesitated long enough for Evie to come to her own conclusion. "Rory was right. I can't believe it." She swore beneath her breath as her arms fell to her sides. "I can't believe how I went on and on about how much I want to run Hillcrest House and you didn't say one word about trying to buy it out from under me!"

Her lack of faith in him stung more than he wanted to admit. "Look, Evie, this isn't Monopoly," he pointed out, an edge of sarcasm to his words. "Just because I land in a certain hotel, that doesn't automatically mean it's going to be swallowed up by the evil James empire. My father heard the hotel might be up for sale, but I'm telling you, Hillcrest House doesn't fit the James brand."

"Hillcrest is a gorgeous hotel! The location, the history behind this building—"

"Do you *want* us to buy the place?" he cut in.

Evie snapped her mouth shut. He could practically hear her molars grinding together before she said, "It's—it's a money pit. Bad investment all around."

"That's what I thought." A wry smile curved his lips. "And I will tell you the same thing I told my father when I was here two months ago."

He reached out again, this time resisting her meager

efforts to pull away as he grasped her shoulders and drew her closer. The thin material of her shirt slid over the silken skin beneath, and Griffin felt the pull of desire tighten his gut.

She kept her face stubbornly averted, but he didn't let that stop him. He tilted his head until she gave a sigh and rolled her eyes in his direction. "Evie McClaren is the most hardheaded, stubborn, determined woman that I have ever met, and she is not going to give up without a fight. Her aunt will never sell Hillcrest House as long as she has anything to say about it."

"You said that?"

"I did."

Her lashes lowered as if he'd lavished her with the most flowery, over-the-top compliments. That mix of confidence and insecurity drew him in, fascinating him as much as the contrast of her blunt-cut dark hair blowing across her smooth cheek.

Unable to resist, he tucked a stray strand behind her ear, running his fingertip across skin the entire way and feeling his blood heat as a flush of color rose in its wake. He drew in a deep breath of cool ocean-damp air, but the scent combined with Evie's warm vanilla and spice only added to the desire burning in his veins.

The longing intensified as her tongue darted out to lick her upper lip, and he could almost taste the sweetness of her kiss, revel in the softness of her lips against his own...

Feminine voices rang out as the lobby doors swung open and some of the women from the bridal shower—Alexa and Rory included—stepped onto the porch. They were laughing as they pushed a brass luggage cart loaded with presents and decorated with a dozen silver and blue balloons. The laughter faded into whispers as they caught sight of Griffin and Evie huddled together in the far corner.

Her attention cut toward her cousin before she looked back at him. "If we're, um, going to stick with the plan and make them think we're dating, maybe we should…" The words trailed off but her eyes finished the unspoken thought as they locked on his lips.

If Evie needed the protection of his pretending to be her fake boyfriend to feel safe, then Griffin would gladly take on that role. He leaned closer, giving in to the urge to bury his fingers in the warm cascade of her hair. His pulse pounded in his ears and every muscle in his body tensed with the need to feel her body pressed tight to his own.

He would play his part, but only so far.

"Evie, Evie, Evie." Her dark-lashed eyes widened and her breath caught as he bent his head to murmur, "When I kiss you for the first time, there won't be an audience… and there will be nothing pretend about it."

Chapter Five

When I kiss you for the first time...there will be nothing pretend about it.

Though the drive into Clearville didn't take more than fifteen minutes, Evie kept her attention laser focused on the phone in her hand. Not that her mind was actually on the dozens of messages popping up faster than she could respond to them. But she needed some kind of distraction from the man behind the wheel.

The luxury car was clearly a rental, a recent enough model to still hold on to a hint of leather and new-car smell. But combining with that was Griffin's cologne—a scent she recalled all too easily from their turn around the tiny dance floor. The slightest whiff and she might as well have been back in his arms again with the possessive feel of his arm around her waist, the tempting brush of his chest against her breasts, the seduction of his thigh between her own...

Griffin had adjusted the thermostat due to the cool temperatures outside, and as much as she would have liked to blame that for the heat burning in her cheeks, she couldn't. She knew that fire was of her own making.

She still couldn't believe she'd practically begged Griffin to kiss her.

Or that he'd actually turned her down.

She'd seen the desire turning his golden eyes molten... hadn't she? It wouldn't be the first time she'd totally misread a man. She would have loved a hole in the earth to hide in; barring that, she'd bury her head in work instead. But even as she concentrated on the phone in her hand, she caught glimpses of Griffin out of the corner of her eye. His perfect profile, his casual, confident grip on the wheel. When he reached over with his right hand, her heart actually skipped a beat even though he was doing nothing more than changing the radio station.

Evie almost groaned at the slow, sexy strains humming from the speakers. Honestly, what were the odds?

"They're playing our song."

"I don't know that one dance is enough to make this ours."

"Sometimes one dance is all it takes, Evie."

It was a silly, flirty, Griffin-type of thing to say, but if Evie didn't know better—if she were willing to give in to the scent and sound combining to work against her— she might have believed every word.

Evie had stopped believing in fairy tales years ago, however. Finding out her fiancé was nothing but a fraud had burst any bubbles of belief naively floating around in her head. In its place had come a hardened skepticism that had her questioning everyone—most especially the man sitting in the seat next to her.

So what if he's flirting? This was all a game to him,

and that was okay. As long as Evie ended up winning Hillcrest House in the end.

"We're here."

Evie glanced out the window and frowned at the red-and-white-striped awning fluttering over Rolly's Diner. A winter scene complete with a top hat–wearing snowman decorated the large windows fronting the restaurant. "My car is parked at the bar, remember?"

She barely had a chance to finish the question before Griffin slid out from behind the wheel. He circled around the car to open her door, and her breath caught in her throat as he bent down to hold out his hand. She'd done her best to avoid looking directly at him, and now, hit with the full force of his golden good looks, she might as well have been staring straight into the sun. She blinked to try to reset her senses, but Griffin was still there. Still gorgeous and extending his hand as if they were about to attend some red-carpet event.

"Why are we here?" she demanded, her voice sharper than she'd intended as his fingers closed around hers and a seductive shiver raced down her spine.

"Because it's time for lunch."

"I already ate at Alexa's shower." Along with the cake, Debbie Pirelli had brought a fruit salad and dozens of bite-size sandwiches. Not that Evie had taken more than a nibble or two.

"Well, I didn't. You aren't going to make me eat alone, are you? That would certainly give everyone something to talk about," he pointed out. "Me sitting all alone after our night of passion. Honestly, Evie, you really need to work on your morning-after routine."

"Not all of us have a routine." And even though their night had been strictly imaginary—for the most part—

she didn't like thinking about all the morning-after women who had come before her.

Griffin grinned. "Then let me show you how it's done."

"You are impossible," she complained even as she allowed him to lead her toward the old-fashioned diner that promised mouthwatering, calorie-filled comfort food. The midday Sunday crowd was a mix of tourists and locals out for last-minute Christmas shopping, and she caught more than one speculative glance at the possessive arm he had wrapped around her waist.

Realizing this lunch was bound to be a rehash of the bridal shower with everyone watching and whispering, Evie stopped short on the sidewalk. Griffin spun her out of the way to keep a couple of teenagers behind them from running her down, and somehow she ended up staring up at him, her palms on his chest and his hands bracketing her hips. "This is a bad idea," she murmured.

Griffin smiled at that. "Don't worry. Bad ideas are my strong suit."

And business was hers. Maybe if she focused on Hillcrest House, on her plan, she wouldn't notice the way a faint dimple flashed in his cheek when he grinned, or how his spicy aftershave drifted over her on the morning air, or how that same cool breeze had brushed a lock of hair over his forehead, tempting the neat freak inside her to push it back.

Catching her completely off guard, he pressed a quick kiss to her cheek before saying, "I'll check with the hostess to see how long the wait is for a table," and walking off as if he hadn't just kissed her. Or as if kissing her was the most natural, commonplace thing in the world...instead of something that was enough to throw her world completely off balance.

She lifted a hand to her lips where the tingle there spread out like wings, unleashing a flurry of butterflies in her stomach. All from such a short, sweet kiss...

The sound of someone calling her name snapped her out of her stupor, and Evie turned to see Chance striding toward her.

"Here comes the groom." The slight tease wasn't enough to ease the frown from her cousin's handsome face. "What's wrong? Something with the wedding—"

He shook his dark head. "I heard you left the bar with Griffin James last night, but I really didn't want to believe it."

Ah, the joys of small-town grapevines. "It's not what you think. Griffin isn't interested in the hotel."

"The hotel? I'm not talking about the hotel. Look, I know Griffin is Alexa's best friend, and I...appreciate that he was there for her when I wasn't."

Chance's jaw clenched at the memory. Evie knew his romance with Alexa hadn't had the easiest beginning. After a weekend fling, Chance had left Alexa to take a photo assignment half a world away. It had been Griffin, and not Chance, Alexa had turned to when she found out she was pregnant.

"You know there was nothing romantic between Griffin and Alexa," Evie argued, ignoring that she'd had some doubts of her own.

"He's been a good friend to her, but that doesn't make him a good boyfriend." Concern drew Chance's eyebrows together as he asked, "Has he told you about the conditions of his trust?"

Evie crossed her arms over her chest. "So that's what you think? That Griffin needs some ulterior motive to be interested in me?"

"That's insulting, McClaren."

Evie glanced over her shoulder as Griffin stepped up behind her.

Chance gave a slight scoffing laugh. "Yeah, well, forgive me for hurting your feelings."

"I'm not talking about my feelings. I'm talking about you and the apology you owe your cousin. Evie is a bright, beautiful, stubbornly fascinating woman. And no man on earth, myself included, would need some asinine hidden motive to spend time with her."

The butterflies that had barely stilled in her stomach took flight again at Griffin's immediate defense. Not that she needed anyone to defend her, but it was…nice that he had. Just the kind of thing a boyfriend should do. Had she been looking for a boyfriend. Which she wasn't. Her cousins had it all wrong. If anyone had an ulterior motive for using someone…

Turning back to her cousin, she insisted, "Chance, I appreciate your concern, but I'm a big girl and I can take care of myself."

The words did little to ease his frown, and she knew exactly what he was thinking. How she'd said those same words when her family had questioned if Eric was the right guy for her. She'd been so certain, so sure that he was exactly the man he'd been pretending to be.

But this, this was different. This time she was the one pretending, and as long as she didn't forget that she was fooling her family and start fooling herself, everything would work out exactly as planned.

"About Chance and Rory…"

Once they were seated in a retro booth with red vinyl seats, Evie leaned over the small table separating them as if the whole diner might be listening in over the piped-in holiday tunes. From what Griffin could tell, the other patrons were more interested in diving into the juicy burgers and salty fries than in any conversation going on around them. Not that Griffin cared what any of the crowd at Rolly's Diner heard or said about him.

But if whatever Evie had to say was so private that she felt the need to lean close enough for him to see the indigo flecks in her eyes and a hint of freckles on the bridge of her nose and to breathe in the faint scent of floral yet spicy notes from her skin…well, then he was all for sharing secrets.

"This whole thing must seem like it's totally out of the blue," she was saying. Or, at least, that was the gist of what Griffin caught once he dragged his attention away from the pale pink lips a salt and pepper shaker away from his own.

"Griffin? Are you listening to anything I'm saying?" she demanded.

"Yeah, sure. Something about your family."

That must have been close enough, because Evie continued, "You need to give them a break when it comes to—" A hint of embarrassed color filled her cheeks, hiding her intriguing freckles, as she waved a hand between them.

Griffin lifted the laminated menu from the table and gave it a puzzled glance. "I have to give them a break when it comes to Rolly's menu?"

Evie snatched it from his hand. "When it comes to… us. This pseudo relationship between us."

"Ah, that." Griffin wasn't sure how much Evie remembered from the night before, but he'd been very clear that whatever was happening between them was anything but pretend. Still, he supposed he had given the fake-boyfriend factor some credence by playing up the morning-after scene for her aunt and cousin. If Evie was more comfortable pretending the attraction between them wasn't real… Well, he was willing to play along with that. For now.

Her lips parted but whatever she might have said was lost in the moment as a waitress swooped by the table to drop off two glasses of ice water. The fortysomething woman's expression lit as she caught sight of Griffin. "Mr. James, so good to have you with us again."

Remembering the woman from his previous visit, he returned her smile. "It's good to be back, Nadine. How's Will doing in school?"

Nadine's smile revealed a motherly pride as she said, "He's keeping his grades up. I think his attendance has more to do with a girl he's met than an actual interest in his classes, but I'll take what I can get."

After reciting the daily specials, the waitress promised to be back for their orders in a minute. Griffin turned his attention back to Evie to find her staring at him in something akin to amazement. "I've lived here for months, and yet somehow you know more about the locals than I do."

Griffin shrugged. "It's not that hard. Everyone has a story. The easiest way to get people to open up is to reveal something of yourself."

A small grin lit Evie's features, teasing him with its warmth before bursting into a full-on smile. "Is that what you were doing this morning?"

Griffin let out a bark of laughter at how much of himself he'd *revealed*. "Hey, it worked, didn't it? After all, I got you to reveal that, hidden behind that serious facade, you have a wicked sense of humor…and that you have a beautiful smile."

Her dark lashes lowered, hiding her thoughts, and Nadine returned before he could say anything more. Griffin placed an order for a roast beef on rye with the potato salad before adding, "And Evie will have…"

"I told you I already ate at the shower." When he pinned her with a knowing look, she admitted, "Sort of ate. Okay, fine. I'll take half a turkey sandwich on wheat, no mayo, and a salad with ranch on the side."

"There, that wasn't so hard was it?" he asked once the waitress walked away.

"No, but I really need to get back to work."

"I don't think it will kill you if you eat lunch away from your desk just this once."

"How do you know where I eat lunch?"

"What can I say? I'm an observant guy." And Evie was nothing if not consistent. She'd had the Hillcrest kitchen deliver lunch to her office every day during his last trip to Clearville.

"You make it a habit to observe the eating habits of virtual strangers?"

"I make it a habit to observe the eating habits of a woman I'm interested in."

Judging by Evie's automatic eye roll, she wasn't ready to take the attraction he'd felt from the moment they met seriously, and he wasn't ready to lay his cards on the well-worn white-flecked Formica table, either. So he turned the conversation to the town's upcoming winter events, including something he'd read about called Holly and Vine.

"It's a first-time event with a small group of vendors and local wineries playing off the holiday theme. But if the night is as successful as everyone hopes, it will become an annual festival."

"And Hillcrest House will have a booth there?"

Evie nodded. "We'll be cross-promoting with Debbie by giving away some of her mini cupcakes and hopefully encouraging futures guests and couples to stay at the hotel or consider Hillcrest as a possible location for their weddings."

As Evie talked about name recognition and the research she'd done, tracking how the number of people on their mailing list and online traffic equated to hotel bookings, Griffin was struck by the realization that he could have had the same conversation at a lunch meeting with his father. But while those meetings tended to bore the life out of him, he was fascinated by how Evie's mind worked.

And while Griffin feared his father would gladly work himself to death, Evie's face glowed with energy and excitement. "Sounds like you've put a lot of work into this event."

"Well, anything for Hillcrest House."

"Right," he said wryly, reminding himself that for Evie, pretending to date him fell into the *anything* category.

Her thoughts seemed to take the same track as she returned to the subject of her family and their reaction to her *pseudo relationship with him*. "Look, the thing is, I haven't exactly had the best track record when it comes to dating."

"Everyone makes mistakes, Evie. You can't tell me neither of your cousins had troubled relationships in the past." Griffin didn't know about Rory, but he was well aware that Chance had almost been stupid enough to let Alexa slip through his fingers.

A slight frown puckered her forehead. "I never really thought of it that way." Griffin wasn't surprised. Evie struck him as the type to always be harder on herself than on those around her. "But still, that's different."

"Different how?"

"Everything worked out for them in the end."

The admission should have sounded positive—a resounding endorsement for true love conquering all. But Griffin heard the underlying pain and the words she didn't say: *everything worked out for them...but not for me.*

He didn't know what had happened in Evie's past relationship with her questionable boyfriends and sensed now wasn't the time to ask. Instead, he reached for her hand resting on top of the laminated menu. He slid his thumb over the delicate ridges of her knuckles and watched as her lips parted in a silent breath. "What if I told you that this time everything's going to work out for you?"

"You mean...with the hotel? With convincing my aunt I can have a life and run Hillcrest?"

A hint of desperation underscored the words. Because she wanted to believe what she was saying, or because she wanted to believe that was what *he* was saying? Griffin gave her hand a tender squeeze. "Sure, Evie. That, too. After all," he said, raising his chin with a pointed glance to the mistletoe hanging overhead, "it is the season for miracles."

Chapter Six

*A*nother step in her plan.

By the following morning, Evie had regained her perspective when it came to her "relationship" with Griffin. Over several cups of strong black coffee, she'd researched the new James hotel in Dubai. The building was a modern marvel, attracting worldwide attention with its futuristic architecture, cutting-edge design and first-class amenities—from a stunning marina to equestrian facilities, to private butler service. All further cementing her confidence that Griffin couldn't possibly be interested in Hillcrest House.

She was doing the right thing in following the path to success her aunt had set out for her. Family, friends, fun, falling in love. Okay, not everything had gone according to plan, but she could adapt. Griffin would be the perfect date for Chance and Alexa's Christmas Eve wedding along with the gala on New Year's Eve. All she had to do was find a way to keep her attraction to Griffin under control for five more days and to remember that he was simply another box to be marked off on her to-do list.

Not that she was actually going to *do* Griffin James. She was just—

"Ugh!"

Frustrated, Evie pressed her hands against her temples as if she could squeeze out the riot of images assailing her, from Griffin's too-sexy smile to the annoying, aggravating, arousing way he had of stealing into her thoughts. She'd barely slept a wink the previous night, tossing and turning as she relived the nothing of a kiss that had almost had her begging for more.

"Computer problems again?"

"What?" Evie blinked at Trisha Katzman. She'd been so caught up in *not* thinking about Griffin, she hadn't noticed the other woman ducking her head inside the office door.

Trisha had been her aunt's right-hand woman and, at first, had resented the cousins' presence. But Trisha's attitude had improved as Rory had once again shown her ability to reach even the most resistant of people, convincing Evie to offer the woman added responsibility and increasing confidence in her role at Hillcrest House.

"I can call for service if we need a tech to take a look," Trisha offered.

As much as she would have liked to blame technology for her current problem, Evie shook her head. "No, the computer's fine. I'm afraid the problem is user error."

"You do seem a bit...distracted. Maybe you should take a break."

"A break?" Evie never took breaks. She was the one who covered for other people, who filled in when employees called in sick. "No, I'm fine. I just need to focus."

There. Another F-word to add to her plan. Proving to her aunt that she had a life outside work was all fine and dandy, but when she was at work, Hillcrest needed to be her top priority.

"Well, maybe these will pick you up." Stepping farther into the doorway, Trisha held out an enormous floral array boasting an unusual mix of fragrant wildflowers and a few familiar leafy green stems with papery bright fuchsia blossoms.

"Those are gorgeous." Evie didn't think she'd seen bougainvillea in an arrangement before. "But I didn't order any additional flowers."

Thanks to Rory, the hotel was overflowing with an abundance of holiday decorations, including small pine trees and vibrant red poinsettias on every flat surface. Extra flowers were the last thing Hillcrest House needed.

Trisha grinned as she set the cut-glass vase on Evie's desk. "These aren't for the hotel. They're for you."

"For me?" Evie asked in surprise.

"Aren't you going to see who they're from?"

"I'll check the card later." Later when she didn't have an eager audience. Later when she could let herself smile like the fool she likely was over the ridiculousness of Griffin James sending her flowers.

"Let me guess," Trisha teased. "From *The Wild Rose*?"

Evie had never been a huge fan of the floral names for the guest rooms. The incongruity of Griffin as a wild rose did nothing to lessen her mortification. She'd realized she wouldn't be able to keep her relationship with Griffin a secret from the employees. But she was Hillcrest's CFO, someone who was supposed to set an example, not some celebrity whose newest hookup was the subject for tabloid fodder.

She opened her mouth, ready to snap that Trisha had

better things to do than speculate over Evie's love life, when Griffin's mellow voice seemed to whisper in her ear.

Everyone has a story.

Evie knew little about her employees' lives. But as Trisha reached out to run her fingers across the soft petals of a bright yellow gerbera daisy, Evie couldn't help wondering. How long it had been since the other woman had received flowers? Was it really so bad for her to want to live vicariously through Evie's relationship?

"Look, Trisha, Griffin James is…" Evie wasn't sure she had the vocabulary to describe the man, so she settled for what was relevant. "He's a Hillcrest guest, so I would appreciate it if you—"

The redhead held up a hand. "Say no more." Miming turning a key at her lips, she vowed, "Mum's the word."

Trisha made the promise just in time as Rory stepped into the office. "Nice flowers. Very unusual."

Her cousin cocked a questioning eyebrow at Evie, but before she could respond, Trisha chimed in. "They are, aren't they? Nina's trying out some new arrangements and wanted to see what Evie thought."

Trisha shot her a conspirator's wink from behind Rory's back before she backed out of the office, and Evie couldn't help but grin. She knew she had a reputation as a tough boss, and that conversation could have gone in a completely different direction, but she thought she'd handled it well.

She glanced at the flower arrangement.

All thanks to Griffin.

"I got a call from Sally," Rory said as she settled into the chair across from Evie's desk. "She said you haven't been in to try on your bridesmaid's dress yet."

"I gave her my size. I'm sure it will be fine."

"Evie." A chiding note entered her cousin's voice.

"It's a bridesmaid's dress. You don't want it looking like something you bought off the rack. We have Sally on standby in case she has to alter Alexa's gown—again—to accommodate the baby on board. I don't want her to have to scramble to fit you in as well, during the holiday rush."

Rory had been after Evie to stop by the dress shop for weeks. If she kept making excuses, her cousin would know why. But she couldn't let this be about her own nonwedding. Five minutes to try on the dress, and she could mark the task off her to-do list. "Fine, I'll go later today."

"Thank you." After a pause, Rory leaned forward and added, "I want to apologize for yesterday. I know I came down kind of hard about Griffin and his family's interest in the hotel…but it's not just the hotel I'm worried about. You haven't even dated in months, and now to jump into a relationship with a man like Griffin James? You're moving so fast. Rushing into this with your heart instead of your head…"

Just like you did with Eric.

Evie *had* rushed into that relationship. And she *had* ignored her cousins' warnings, their advice, their concern… Feeling like they were forcing her to choose between them and the man she loved, Evie had chosen Eric. A decision that had driven a wedge between her and her cousins that lingered to this day.

It was a distance that had started to close as they'd worked together at the hotel; and one Evie hoped to erase by convincing her aunt not to sell the tangible link that held them all together.

Her faux relationship with Griffin was supposed to be helping in that endeavor, not driving a deeper wedge.

What was that expression about needing to stop digging once you were already in over your head? And yet she heard herself say, "Griffin isn't Eric. And I'm not the same foolish girl I was two years ago."

"You weren't foolish. You were in love. You *deserve* to be in love, and if you don't think Griffin is that man—"

"Not everyone falls in love at first sight, Rory. Griffin and I are…having fun." Evie resisted the urge to duck, certain lighting might strike any moment. But as the atmosphere above her desk remained clear, she realized the words weren't a complete fabrication.

How many times that morning had she found herself fighting a smile as she thought of Griffin's audacity when he stepped out of the bathroom and greeted her aunt wearing nothing more than a hand towel and a smile? Okay, so she'd been horrified at the time, but how better to show her aunt that Evie had a life and a man of her own?

"Fun?" Rory echoed as if she were the one who'd never heard the word before.

Fighting that smile again, Evie said, "Yeah, fun."

Griffin was a means to an end, and as long as she kept that in mind, she'd survive these next few weeks. She'd convince her aunt that she could have a life and Hillcrest House, too, and Griffin would go back to Dubai or some other faraway, exotic locale. She'd keep up the pretense of the relationship for a little while after he left, and then they'd call it quits, the long distance too much to overcome.

She had a plan, and her plans always worked as long as she stayed the course.

Bolstered by the internal pep talk, Evie ignored the mocking voice reminding her that Griffin James was hardly one to follow the rules.

* * *

Griffin stepped into his suite following a morning run on the beach to the sound of his phone vibrating on the coffee table. The muscles that had started to ease into a relaxed state of exhaustion instantly tightened at the sound.

Running his hands through his damp hair, he glared at the phone. He'd been ignoring his father's almost constant calls since he arrived in Clearville and was tempted to avoid this one, as well. He didn't want anything to distract from his thoughts of Evie. What were his chances of sharing that kiss he'd promised her the next time they met?

He'd looked for her in the lobby that morning, but her office door had been closed. He wondered if she received the flowers and what she thought of his special request to add the bougainvillea to the arrangement. The more time they spent together, the more she reminded him of the beautiful but prickly plant.

The combination intrigued him, but he needed to take care and remember that Evie had those thorns for a reason. In working his way past her defenses, he had seen more and more of the vulnerability she fought to hide and figured she'd been hurt badly enough to build up that sharp-witted defense.

After wiping his sweaty forehead against the sleeve of his sweatshirt, he reached for the phone. If he didn't answer, the damn thing would continue to buzz and he might as well get the status report over with.

"What's the latest on Hillcrest House?" Frederick James demanded by way of greeting.

Another time, his father's single-minded focus on business would have spiked an all too familiar surge of resentment. But at the moment, the straight-to-the-point attitude suited Griffin. "Status quo. I told you before, the cousins aren't interested in selling."

Walking over to the refrigerator in the tiny kitchenette, he pulled out a sports drink and cracked the lid off the cold plastic bottle. He took a large swallow, the orange-flavored liquid tart against his tongue.

"But they aren't the ones making the decision, right?" his father was saying. "Their aunt owns the hotel."

"She does, but I don't get the impression she's all that involved in the business." A sound came across the line—a half snort, half choke. "You all right, Dad?"

Clearing his throat, Frederick sounded far more like himself as he barked out, "Fine. Fine. But what makes you think Evelyn—Ms. McClaren—is no longer the one in charge?"

"Yesterday was the first time I've seen her around the hotel. I get the feeling she's looking to hand over the reins to her nieces." And Evie was raring to grab hold. "Maybe she's ready to retire."

"Retire!" His father bounced the word back like a hundred-mile-an-hour volley. "That's ridiculous. That doesn't sound like the woman I—I remember at all."

"Wait..." Pieces started to fall into place and Griffin thought he was getting a better picture of why his father was so interested in the hotel. He set his drink on the small dining room table. "I get it now. She's the one that got away, isn't she?"

Silence filled the end of the line for so long that Griffin thought they'd been disconnected. "Dad? You still there?"

"I'm here."

"So am I right? Is Hillcrest House the one that got away? The one deal you couldn't close?"

"It was—it was a long time ago, but yes, that's certainly one way to put it," Frederick mused. "The one who got away."

Griffin gave a small laugh as his steps carried him across the small suite. He never would have imagined his father as the sentimental type. Frederick James was more "take charge" and "full steam ahead." Looking back— or even slowing down—were concepts reserved for the competition he left in the dust.

"You're going to have to give up on this one," Griffin advised as he dropped onto the floral-patterned sofa. "You have no idea how far Evie's willing to go to hang on to the hotel." Though he tried to keep his voice matter-of-fact and businesslike, he couldn't quite keep the hint of amusement from creeping in as he thought of Evie suggesting that he kiss her—just for show, of course. He'd had a hell of a time not giving in, but he meant what he'd told her.

When he kissed her, there would be nothing pretend about it.

"Stubborn, is she?" his father asked.

"You don't know the half of it. Stubborn and smart… and funny, even though she doesn't even seem to realize it." Just as she didn't seem to realize her own beauty. She wasn't elegantly beautiful like Alexa or even sweetly pretty like her cousin Rory. No… Evie—Evie had a striking kind of beauty that was truly her own.

Griffin didn't know how long he'd been talking before he caught himself. Jeez, he sounded like a teenager suffering in the throes of his first crush. But even as a teenager, he'd never talked to his father about girls. By the time he'd turned fourteen, it seemed that he and his father never talked at all, the silence left behind by his mother's death too much for either of them to fill.

"After the wedding…" his father began, and Griffin's

hand clenched around the phone. If Hillcrest fell off his father's radar, there would be no reason for Griffin to stay in town. No doubt his dad would want him on a plane headed overseas as soon as Alexa and Chance said "I do."

"…I think you should stick around Clearville."

Griffin blinked, sitting up straight at the last words he expected to hear. "You do?"

"I know you feel certain that this Evie isn't interested in selling, but from everything I've heard, her aunt is. And if she does…"

His father's voice trailed off, and this time Griffin felt like his stomach had taken a plunge off the forty-seventh story of the James Tower in Dubai. He'd sworn to Evie that his father wasn't interested in Hillcrest House. If she couldn't convince her aunt not to sell and if his father was the one to buy the hotel—

Evie would never forgive him. In her eyes, he would have betrayed her in the worst possible way…even though everything else he'd told her was completely true. Hillcrest still didn't fit the James brand, but if the Victorian was some great white whale from his father's past, then there was no telling how far Frederick James would go to win it at last.

"Dad…" Griffin heard the strangled sound of his own voice as the truth lodged in his throat. He was tempted to tell his father everything—about how incredible Evie was, about how much she loved the hotel, about how losing it would destroy her and might ruin him in the process.

But the very concept of spilling his guts to his father was so foreign, so unheard-of, that he couldn't say the words. He didn't want to pour out his feelings only to have his dad break into his typical speech. The oft repeated and oh-so-tired tirade about how Griffin needed to focus on business, to keep his head in the game, eyes on the prize. His father would never understand that, for the first time in years, Griffin's head, his eyes, his whole damn body was right where he needed to be.

Still, for Evie, he had to try. He launched into a litany of all the hotel's problems—the out-of-the-way locale, the old-fashioned vibe, the slow-paced, small-town feel. Despite his certainty that Hillcrest House wasn't a fit for their company, he had done his homework. But all the bullet points he listed, all the hotel's supposed disadvantages, were the very things that made Hillcrest special. That made it as unique and beautiful as Evie...

"I don't know what happened before, but you're not going to have any better luck this time around," Griffin said finally, hoping his father had listened, really listened, to—hell, to everything he *wasn't* saying.

He should have known better than to expect his father to hear anything at all.

"Maybe I won't," Frederick pointed out. "But maybe this time *you* will."

Chapter Seven

Evie had never been in A Stitch in Time, the bridal shop on Main Street. Housed in one of the town's many converted Victorians, the store clung to its romantic past with elegantly posed mannequins draped in satin and lace in the silver-bell-decorated front window.

While Evie would admit the dresses were gorgeous, she couldn't get past the impracticality. All the time and money and effort spent on one day. A day that, in her case, had never come. Which might have had something to do with her reluctance to step inside the vanilla-and-rose-scented shop.

The bell over the door was still tinkling as she heard Sally gush, "Perfect. Just perfect!"

Standing in the middle of the shop, the woman was not speaking to a blushing bride-to-be, but to a broad-shouldered man in a gorgeous tuxedo. Griffin turned at the sound of the bell, a slow grin forming as he caught sight of her. "Evie, darling, what an unexpected pleasure."

"And such good timing." Sally beamed. "I have your dress right here." The brown-haired woman grabbed a bright pink plastic-wrapped hanger off a rack behind the desk. "It will be a preview of the wedding!"

Sally sighed as an employee called her name from the back of the store. "Do not leave without me seeing how that dress fits," she warned before disappearing down a narrow hallway and leaving Evie holding the bag.

The plastic crinkled as she pressed the dress to her stomach, hoping to calm the riot of nerves dancing inside. "So…I would have thought you'd have a custom-made tuxedo on hand."

"Oh, I do, but Alexa wanted all the groomsmen to match."

Evie swallowed a snort. It wasn't going to happen. No way would the other men in the bridal party look anywhere near as good in their tuxes as Griffin did in his.

"So," he said, tilting his head toward the dressing room. "It's all yours."

Evie tightened her grip on the garment bag as her nerves took another turn, this time nose-diving in a sickening spiral. Ever since her broken engagement, the mere thought of weddings and walking down the aisle made her sick to her stomach.

Every borrowed, blue, old and new tradition slapped at her in reminders of how foolish she'd been, how readily and gullibly she'd fallen for all of Eric's lies. Little wonder she'd put off coming to the bridal shop filled with promises of forever that were as substantial as the fragile lace and strings of seed pearls holding them all together.

But she wasn't about to let tuxedo-wearing Griffin James know she was freaked out by formal wear. Marching across the small shop, she swept the pink curtain aside and stepped inside the dressing room. She fought a groan at the mirrored walls, reflecting every possible angle back at her.

"How's it going in there?"

Evie gritted her teeth at the cheery sound of Griffin's voice on the other side of the curtain. A curtain she had to remind herself that he could not see through. So why did slipping out of her sensible shoes and sliding her slacks down her legs make her feel like she was stripping in front of him?

"You know, you really don't have to wait around for this."

"Oh, come on, I showed you mine…" Now a seductive note entered his voice, and Evie had to stop herself from reaching for the material pooling around her ankles and covering up once more. Because while Griffin might not have X-ray vision, she had the feeling he still somehow knew exactly how rattled she was by the whole experience.

"Stepping out of my bathroom in nothing but a towel was your idea. Not mine."

His husky laughter reverberated through the shop, and Evie was surprised the deep, sexy sound wave didn't have the curtain at her back trembling on its metal hooks.

"I was talking about you seeing me in my tux. But anytime you want to show me more—or should I say less?—than you in that bridesmaid's dress, just say the word, sweetheart."

Evie's muffled curse as she stripped her sweater over her head had him laughing once more.

"Not the word I was expecting."

"Honestly, you are impossible. Do you ever take anything seriously?"

"I am completely serious about you."

Evie rolled her eyes at her own reflection. Another

flirtatious response. Had she expected something more? *Just try on the dress and get this over with.* She whisked the zipper down the garment bag and froze.

Alexa had sent pictures of the style she had in mind several weeks ago. Other than providing Sally with her measurements, Evie had given the sleeveless icy-blue sheath little thought. Like any other bridesmaid's dress, it would be worn once and then forgotten.

So what was it now about the liquid shimmer of satin that had her reaching out and carefully withdrawing the long skirt from the bag? Why was her breath catching at the intricate beauty of the seed pearls and lace embellishing the neckline? Why did the thought of slipping the garment over her head have her heart racing in anticipation?

"Evie? You do know you have to come out sometime, don't you?"

Swallowing hard, she slid the bodice from the padded hanger. Yes, she knew she would have to step outside the dressing room at some point. And that made all the difference. Not that she would be wearing the dress...but who she would be wearing it for.

The satin slid like a whisper over her skin—a brush against her breasts, belly and thighs. She could tell immediately that the dress would fit like a dream—the straight skirt highlighting her height and the fitted bodice adding a bit of lift to her somewhat meager cleavage.

Evie twisted her arms behind her only to blow out a frustrated breath when the zipper stopped midway up her back. She tried reaching up over her shoulder to grasp the tiny tab, but still no go.

Pulling the zipper down didn't work, either. What were the odds that she, of all people, would be stuck wearing a bridesmaid's dress for the rest of her life?

"Seriously?" she huffed, loud enough, evidently, for Griffin to overhear.

"Having trouble in there?"

"Is Sally back yet?"

"Nope. It's just me out here. Why? What's wrong?"

"The zipper's stuck."

Griffin was silent for a moment before his chuckle danced down her bare back. "Lucky for you, I do have some experience with stubborn zippers."

"No doubt. But I'm sure that experience has more to do with undressing than dressing women." Evie tugged at the zipper again, but other than feeling like she was about to dislocate her shoulder, she had no more success. "I give up. Can you—"

Before she could finish her request for Griffin to track down the seamstress, the curtain behind her parted. Only it wasn't Sally who stepped through. "Griffin! What are you doing?"

His eyebrow rose as he met her gaze in one of the many mirrors. "You said you needed help."

"Not from you!" She whirled to face him, the loose bodice clutched to her chest. The tiny dressing room was cramped to start with. Griffin's masculine presence further shrank the space…until the deep breath she took had the backs of her knuckles brushing against the starched shirtfront of his tuxedo. "You shouldn't be in here."

"Come now, Evie, haven't you noticed yet that rescuing damsels in distress is something of a habit of mine?"

"I'm not a damsel. And I'm not distressed. I'm just—"

"Undressed?" At her narrowed glare, he lifted a hand and spun his index finger in a circle. "Turn around."

Evie hesitated a moment before giving him her back. "Only so I can get this over with."

"Uh-huh. Whatever you say, Evie."

She sucked in a quick breath at the brush of his fingers against her spine. "Be careful," she warned, her voice more of a breathless whisper than strident command. "You don't want to snag the material."

"I told you before, I take very good care of the fine things in my hands."

As promised, the zipper responded to his nimble touch, sliding into place with ease. It should have been her cue to exhale, but with Griffin standing so close, with his image—their images—reflected all around her, she forgot how to breathe. Instead of stepping back now that the job was done, he moved even closer. They stared at each other in the mirror—the emotional intensity in that connection leaving her feeling as exposed as if he'd walked in on her naked—and yet she couldn't look away.

His arm wrapped around her waist, pulling her body closer to the heat and strength of his. Her legs trembled and her head tipped back against his shoulder. All that from the wonderful feel of his mouth drifting to the side of her neck.

"Griffin."

His name was little more than a gasp and his answer little more than a challenging grin. "Yes, Evie?"

Oh, the heck with it.

Stiffening what was left of her spine, she met his challenge with one of her own. "There's no one watching, so why don't you kiss me already?"

"All you had to do was ask."

Evie was barely aware of turning in his arms, but she must have because the next thing she knew, those same talented hands were cupping her face as he lowered his mouth to hers. The desire she'd been denying since Griffin had first shown up at the hotel flared into something out of control. She clutched at his shoulders, desperate to get closer, the seed pearls and beadwork on her bodice scraping against the studs on his shirtfront. Her curves met the hardened planes and angles of his masculine form—softening, conforming, blending with a sense of perfection that made it almost impossible to think, to remember...

And Evie *needed* to think. She had a plan, but in that moment, in his arms, nothing mattered beyond Griffin and the incredible, wonderful way he made her feel.

Her head fell back, her muscles melting under the heat of his kiss as his lips trailed down her throat. Her eyelids fluttered, and she froze as she caught sight of the woman in the mirror, her pupils dark with arousal, a flush of passion staining her skin. This was a reckless woman Evie didn't recognize. Her hands tensed at Griffin's shoulders, but she didn't even need to apply any pressure before he was pulling away.

That he could read her so well, so easily, left Evie feeling even more vulnerable. She stared at Griffin's bow tie, still perfectly straight and perfectly tied while she felt thoroughly undone and out of sorts. Any moment now, Griffin would make some teasing comment that would prove how unaffected he was.

But then she noticed the strong, tanned column of his neck move as he swallowed hard. The ragged, out-of-control breathing wasn't only her own. When she did finally raise her eyes to Griffin's, she didn't need all the mirrors surrounding them to see the molten desire reflected back to her in his golden gaze.

"Tell me, Evie—" his voice deepened on her name,

the sound thrumming like resonant bass notes until she could feel the vibrations straight down to her bones "—does this still feel pretend to you?"

As she sat in her office the next morning, romance was the last thing Evie wanted to think about. She couldn't close her eyes without reliving the sensation of Griffin's lips against hers. Bad enough her simple, straightforward plan was rapidly unraveling in her fingers. Worse was the way she'd practically come apart in his arms.

Does this still feel pretend to you?

Pretend? No, but certainly not *real*, either. A gorgeous man standing behind her in a tuxedo, his lips brushing her cheek as he whispered in her ear? That was all in the wonderful realm of fantasy, the best kind of daydream... As if Evie possessed the kind of imagination to come up with something so deliciously good.

But the momentary distraction only proved she needed to focus more than ever on the hotel and on the job she had to do. Unfortunately, she'd forgotten the purpose of the meeting she had scheduled with her aunt, Trisha and Aaron Braun, the hotel's head chef.

"It's going to be the most romantic New Year's Eve Ball ever!" Trisha exclaimed as she hugged her tablet to her chest.

"That is the idea, isn't it?" Her aunt beamed. "Right, Evie?"

"Right. It's all about the romance," Evie muttered. They'd already spent the first half of the meeting going over details for the Holly and Vine event the following night before moving on to the upcoming gala. "Do you have the final numbers from the food vendors?"

"Because nothing says romance more than invoices from the local butcher shop," her aunt said with a sigh.

Evie winced, recognizing her business-first mistake too late, but was saved from making excuses when Trisha muttered, "I would if *someone* ever finalized the menu."

With that, the tall redhead shot the fourth member of the group gathered in Evie's office a withering look. Their brilliant and temperamental chef glared back. "My contact hasn't been able to guarantee he'd have the mushrooms I need for the risotto," Aaron said. "I can't put mushroom risotto on the menu if I can't get mushrooms."

Trisha threw up a hand. "And the whole state of California is…out of mushrooms?"

"Not just any mushrooms will do," the dark-haired chef stressed.

"Oh, right. Because these are *magic* mushrooms."

Evie barely withheld an annoyed sigh. Ever since they'd hired the new chef a few months back, the two had been at odds. Trisha was responsible for their promotions and social media, and the content on the hotel's culinary offerings was frequently lacking thanks to Aaron's refusal to pin down an exact menu.

"You're right. The way I prepare them is pretty magical!"

Trisha shot back a quick response, and it took everything inside Evie not to snap at both of them. But she had to show her aunt she could manage Hillcrest's personnel as easily as she could manage its finances. If only she didn't want to knock their heads together!

"If you tried it, you'd change your mind," Aaron was arguing, but Trisha gave a short laugh.

"Doubt it. I hate mushrooms. *All* mushrooms."

"Oh, well, in that case, let me revise my entire menu

based on the tastes of a woman who thinks a proper meal is dehydrated noodles microwaved in a foam cup!"

"I like those noodles. Besides," Trisha added, tossing her hair back defiantly, "what do you care what I eat for lunch, anyway?"

Aaron didn't answer, but Evie heard a response loud and clear. *I make it a habit to observe the eating habits of a woman I'm interested in.*

Was it possible? Was their fighting something more than two employees who couldn't get along? Studying the couple, Evie started to wonder. The flush on Trisha's cheeks, the darkening of Aaron's eyes, were those telltale signs of awareness rather than anger?

Last week, when the two were arguing over Aaron's insistence that something was wrong with the state-of-the-art refrigerator, the thought had never crossed her mind. But now...

"Look, you two," she interrupted, "that's a great idea."

They stopped fighting long enough to turn to her in confusion. "What is?"

"To do a test run of the meal," Evie said, as if that was what the two employees had been discussing all along. "Aaron, you can pull out all the stops and see where things go from there."

Silence fell for a tense moment as the two stared at each other across her office. "If I can get the mushrooms," Aaron clarified.

Trisha smiled sweetly. "They sell them in cans now, you know? Want me to pick some up for you the next time I'm shopping for noodle soup?"

"Once you taste my risotto," the chef asserted, "you'll change your mind."

"We'll see, won't we?"

Even though the challenge seemed to reverberate in the air between them, at least now there was something they agreed on. After another few minutes of far more productive discussion, the four of them were able to decide on the potential menu.

"You handled that well," her aunt complimented Evie as they walked out of her office sometime later.

Evie warmed at the praise. She'd hold hands and sing "Kumbaya" if that was what it would take to prove herself to her aunt. "Thanks. I have a feeling that something more than mushrooms is going on between the two of them."

"And you don't disapprove?"

Evie started. "Should I?" A few weeks ago, she most certainly would have. An on-the-job romance was never a good idea. Trisha had worked at the hotel for years and knew the ins and outs better than anyone except for her aunt, and Aaron was an amazing chef. If Hillcrest lost either of them—crap! What had she been thinking, encouraging the two of them to get together for a romantic taste-test dinner? "I should, shouldn't I? With the way the two of them fight now, when they're not dating, what's it going to be like if they break up?"

"And what makes you so sure that's what will happen?" Eyeing her closely, her aunt said, "You know, a long time ago, I felt like I had to make a choice between pursuing my career and following my heart."

"You chose Hillcrest House," Evie stated with certainty.

"I did, and I was always sure I'd made the right choice, but recently I've had time to rethink that decision." Reaching up, Evelyn fingered the flyaway ends of undyed hair, her attention locked in a distant past. Then, with a quick shake of her head, she gave a short laugh.

"Maybe Trisha and Aaron will make it work. Have a whirlwind courtship and fall in love right here at Hillcrest House. You know," her aunt said as she pinned Evie with a look, "just like you and Griffin."

Chapter Eight

"Right." Too stunned by her aunt's revelation, Evie's attempt at an easy, breezy agreement sounded more like she was drowning in quicksand. "Just like me and Griffin."

Her aunt placed a hand on her arm. "Is everything all right between the two of you?" For all her casual clothes and relaxed hairstyle, her aunt was as sharp as ever, and Evie knew.

She was blowing this.

She had the perfect man willing to play her perfect boyfriend, and she was blowing it. Not because her aunt didn't believe it, but because Evie wasn't letting herself believe it. Her aunt would never have been fooled into thinking a man like Wade would be enough to make Evie forget about work, but a man like Griffin James? He was enough to make Evie forget her name, her birthday, where she lived and who she was, as he had so thoroughly and seductively proved in the bridal shop dressing room.

Does this still feel pretend to you?

And the truth was, only by pretending that the attraction, the desire, the emotion *weren't* real did Evie have any hope of protecting herself from the reckless, out-of-control way he made her feel.

Unable to meet her aunt's eyes, she glanced almost wildly around the lobby crowded with holiday guests. She knew every nook and cranny of the walnut-paneled room with its carved columns, coffered ceiling and antique check-in desk, and yet she couldn't recall ever feeling at such a loss.

"We're—" Evie struggled to speak, but then words didn't matter because he was there, striding across the patterned carpet, casually elegant in a gray shirt and black slacks.

"Here he is now," she said to her aunt before calling out his name.

Her cheeks heated as the sound seemed to echo, not through the lobby, but once more through the tiny dressing room, a reminder of how she'd nearly come apart in his arms. She'd known she couldn't avoid him forever after that mind-blowing, soul-stealing kiss, but she wasn't prepared for the jolt of awareness shooting through her as she spotted him.

And though his sexy lips curved into a slight smile, he didn't actually laugh in her face as she hurried toward him…exactly the way a woman in love would.

She stopped short of throwing herself into his arms because he'd already warned her, hadn't he? *When I kiss you, there won't be an audience…and there will be nothing pretend about it.*

"Hey, babe."

Babe? Clearly they needed to talk about pet names and the fact that no one had ever called her babe. And yet she couldn't deny her insides melted a bit at the proprietary claim. When he leaned in to press a kiss against her cheek and murmur, "Missed you," Evie's insides did more than melt. They liquefied like the molten center of one of Aaron's rich and decadent lava cakes.

"Griffin…"

He pulled away before her bones puddled right along with her brains. "Ms. McClaren, good to see you again."

"You, too, even if I'm not seeing quite as much of you," Evelyn said archly.

And now it was embarrassment that had her ready to sink right into the floor. *If I close my eyes, maybe—just maybe—they won't be able to see me at all…*

But when Griffin's deep chuckle took her back to the bridal shop dressing room, to his hands at her zipper and lips warm against her neck, Evie snapped her eyes back open. Her aunt was still watching her with the pinpoint awareness that had her reaching out to grab Griffin's hand and hold on for dear life.

I need this to look real. I need to believe this is real… just for a little while.

As if he could hear every word she'd never said, Griffin brushed a tender kiss against her temple and gave her hand a reassuring squeeze. Swallowing hard, she dared to look up at him and saw the unspoken response in his confident smile. *We've got this, Evie.*

For the first time since the meeting with her aunt a month ago, the tension, the pressure, the weight of responsibility of keeping Hillcrest House in the family started to ease.

We've got this.

"Evie had a wonderful idea during our meeting this morning."

"I'm not surprised. I've told Evie more than once that

she's full of brilliant ideas." Smiling at her aunt, Griffin added, "I'm pretty sure she gets that from you."

"And aren't you the charming one? I suppose we both know where you get *that* from."

Griffin's eyebrows shot toward his hairline at her aunt's comment. Evie didn't have a chance to wonder what her aunt might have meant before the older woman turned toward her. "Aren't you going to tell Griffin your idea?"

Idea? As the memory of their kiss still swirled through her thoughts, Evie wasn't planning on sharing any ideas the sight of him inspired. "Uh, what idea, Aunt E?"

"About taste testing the dinner for the New Year's Eve Ball."

"Oh, right. Our chef has come up with a new menu for the dance, and I thought it would be a great idea to have a preview before the big event." As she caught the expectation in her aunt's expression, she mentally slapped herself upside the head for not figuring it out sooner. Clearly she wasn't as brilliant as either her aunt or Griffin believed.

Taking a deep breath, Evie turned toward Griffin. "Just for the two of us."

Because naturally her aunt hadn't been thinking of Aaron and Trisha when Evie made her suggestion. No, Evelyn had been thinking—

"Who better to judge a romantic dinner than Hillcrest's newest couple?"

"Who indeed?" Griffin agreed.

"I'll leave the two of you to work out the details. I'll expect a full report later." With a sly smile, Evelyn clarified, "On the dinner, that is."

Griffin chuckled as her aunt left them with a wink and a wave. "I'm impressed, Evie. Planning such a romantic evening for us."

"You know me and my plans," she muttered. Considered how far she'd already gone, dinner hardly seemed much of a price to pay. But as she glanced around the lobby with its holly-dotted garlands, enormous pine-scented wreaths and glittering lights, Evie felt like she was seeing the place with different eyes. She'd been so sure Hillcrest House was all her aunt ever wanted. It was all Evie ever wanted, wasn't it?

"Evie?"

Realizing that Griffin was watching her, she shook off the momentary doubt. Of course, Hillcrest was what she wanted, and she'd do whatever she could to hold on to it. Including having that romantic dinner with Griffin James.

"When I brought up the idea, I wasn't exactly thinking of the two of us."

After Evie explained the battle in her office and pointed out the combatants in question before they stalked off to their respective corners, Griffin grinned. "Ah, those two. I don't suppose the hotel has some kind of no-fraternizing policy, does it?"

Evie gaped at him. How had Griffin picked up on something in a single glance that she'd been blind to for months? "How did you—never mind." If he had some kind of superpower when it came to reading auras or sensing pheromones of attraction, well, she definitely did *not* want to know.

"And to answer your question, we don't have a policy against employees dating. Although, it might be a good idea to implement one. Quickly."

Griffin laughed as he took her arm and guided her out of the flow of guests and porters wheeling luggage through the busy lobby. "Why? Surely you don't want to be the one keeping star-crossed lovers apart."

She waved a hand in the direction of the kitchen. "Aaron is a brilliant chef. We're lucky to have someone of his caliber willing to work here in Clearville rather than in Portland or San Francisco. And Trisha's been here for years."

"I'm still not sure I see the problem."

"The problem—" Evie tried to tamp down the cynicism building inside her, but she felt more like a two-year-old stomping her foot in a tantrum as she all but snapped, "The problem is, what happens when the relationship doesn't work out?"

"And maybe the answer is what happens if it does?"

She huffed out a breath. "Soon you'll be telling me all about Hillcrest's magic and how this place brings two hearts together with its blend of romance and blah, blah, blah."

Griffin let out a bark of laughter. "Well, I have heard Rory's speech."

"Right. When you and Alexa were the couple getting married, how'd that work out for you?" Oh, good grief! Had she really said that? And how had the question that sounded like her typical snarky response to love and marriage in her head come out sounding like the words of a jealous girlfriend when spoken out loud?

"Exactly as it was supposed to. I told you before that Alexa's a friend. She and Chance are the ones meant to have their happily-ever-after. But what about you?"

"Me?"

"Yes, Evie, you. Why don't you believe you'll find your one true love?"

Evie opened her mouth to snap back with another sarcastic reply, shocked down to her shoes when the unvarnished truth poured out instead. "Maybe because you aren't the only one whose engagement didn't end with a walk down the aisle."

Griffin had expected some kind of heartbreak in Evie's past. For all her tough-as-nails exterior, she had a heart made for loving. He'd seen it in her interaction with her aunt, in her desire to hold on to Hillcrest House and to keep her family together.

But he hadn't expected a fiancé. Just as he hadn't expected the sudden spike of jealousy, knowing there was a man Evie McClaren had loved enough to want to marry. Even if, in the end, they hadn't made it to the altar.

"The man's an idiot."

"What?"

Griffin didn't realize he'd said the words out loud until he saw Evie staring at him. Her chin was raised to a proud level, head held high, back straight; she was ready to pretend the broken engagement hadn't broken her heart.

"The man's an idiot," he repeated, well aware of what he was saying this time. Well aware his own words might soon come back to bite him. "He'd have to be to lose you."

"Maybe I'm the one who left him," she shot back. "Ever think of that?"

"Then he's still an idiot for not doing everything he could to get you back."

Evie's chest heaved as she drew in a breath, but it was more than anger rushing through her veins. He could see it in the trapped look in her expression. She'd opened the box to the past with her admission, one that he would guess she'd buried deep as she'd thrown herself into her job.

Better with numbers than with people, she'd told him that night at the bar.

But Griffin was willing to bet it wasn't so much that

Evie was better with numbers as it was that she found safety in them. He recognized the signs of someone who buried themselves in work. He'd seen it for years with his father and witnessed it in his own reflection staring back at him lately.

I'm counting on you, Griff. A whisper of memory echoed through his mind, so faded now he could hear the words but no longer remember the sound of his mother's voice. *I'm counting on you to make your dad smile. The way you've always made me smile.*

Griffin had failed to keep his promise. He'd done little to make his father smile over the years since his mother's death. Not that he hadn't tried. He'd followed in Frederick's footsteps. He'd worked his way up through the James Hotels hierarchy, starting at the bottom despite his name, and climbing to the top. But instead of making his father happy, all he'd succeeded in was making himself miserable.

"Come on," he said suddenly as he grabbed Evie's hand. "Let's get some fresh air."

After they'd walked some distance along the gravel path, the crunch of their footsteps and the rustle of salty air in the trees the only sounds, Evie finally said, "My cousins and I used to come here almost every summer. It didn't matter that we had to share the hotel with hundreds of guests. It was ours."

Griffin could easily imagine it. Adventurous, reckless Chance; imaginative, exuberant Rory; and smart, serious Evie—all big eyes, skinny limbs and a shy, sweet smile. The three of them must have explored every inch of the property from the lush, landscaped grounds to the rocky shoreline below.

"It's still yours, Evie," he reminded her even as he vowed to make sure it stayed that way. "You've got a plan, remember? You'll get your chance to run Hillcrest House."

"That's just it. I've already had my chance, and I've already blown it."

"What do you mean?"

For a long moment, he didn't think she was going to answer as she contemplated the clouds rolling in off the ocean. Finally, with her thoughts clearly in the past, she started speaking. "A few years ago, I approached my aunt about buying into Hillcrest. I'd worked my way up at the accounting firm, putting in all the overtime, going after every promotion and major client along the way. But despite my success, I finally hit a glass ceiling at the company and by then I was burned out. I wanted something different, something new. Or maybe something old."

"Hillcrest House."

Evie nodded. "I grew up hearing the stories about how everyone had always known Aunt Evelyn would take over from my grandparents, and I remember thinking how one day that would be me. One day she would pass the keys for the castle on to me."

"What happened?"

Evie's lips twisted in a mockery of the smile he always wanted to see on her face. "I fell in love with Eric Laughlin."

And now the man had a name. Eric Laughlin…which would make it so much easier to track him down and beat the hell out of him, as Griffin felt like doing.

"Eric was charming, sophisticated, handsome…"

Words Griffin had often heard over the years from women describing him. He would never claim to be perfect, but the idea of Evie comparing him to the other man, possibly penalizing him for another man's sins, was yet another reason for the ass kicking in Eric Laughlin's future.

"As things got more serious between us, I thought I'd have to choose between Eric and the hotel. I couldn't imagine him leaving Portland. But then he came to Clearville with me for Christmas, and he said he loved it. Everything about the town and about Hillcrest House. Two months later, he proposed, and suddenly my dream was even better because I was going to have someone by my side."

"Eric." He practically spit the word like a curse, the nastiness of the name on his tongue enough to bring a small smile from Evie.

But the expression faded quickly as she crossed her arms over her chest, to shield herself more from the memories than from the weather. With her chin ducked down against her chest, she looked small, vulnerable, folding in on herself when all Griffin wanted for Evie was to see her spread her wings and soar.

"He said he had this vision of me as a June bride, so I threw myself into planning a wedding in four months… even though Rory and Chance thought I was rushing into things. Both of them had always been the popular ones, going out on dates while I was the one sitting at home with my head buried in a book. Eric was my first…serious relationship."

Pink touched her cheeks, not from the hint of chill on the salt-scented breeze, but from the words she'd left unsaid. Eric had been her first lover.

The very idea was enough to make him want to pull Evie into his arms. To wipe every memory of the other man from her mind, her body, her heart until Griffin was all Evie could see, taste and touch. The raw possessiveness was as out of character as the raging jealousy, powerful emotions Griffin had never allowed himself to feel.

Apparently unaware of the turmoil consuming him, Evie said, "But for all of Rory's and Chance's relationships, I was the first one of us to get engaged. So when they questioned if Eric was really the man for me, I told myself they were jealous that I was the one who'd found true love first.

"I wanted them to be happy for me and instead… Well, it turned out I still did have to choose, and I chose Eric. The wedding plans were moving full speed ahead. I had everything organized down to the tiniest detail—paying a ridiculous amount of attention to the dress, the flowers, the music, the menu—when what I should have been paying more attention to was the man I was marrying."

"But you figured it out, Evie. You didn't marry him."

"Oh, I figured it out all right. A whopping two days before I was supposed to walk down the aisle, I overheard Eric on the phone. He was talking with a lawyer about how long we would have to stay married before he'd be entitled to half of my share of Hillcrest House in a divorce."

Griffin swore beneath his breath, and then again much louder. "That—that's why he was rushing the wedding?"

"That's the only reason he asked me to marry me in the first place." Painful shadows from the past darkened her expression. "To get his hands on Hillcrest House."

Chapter Nine

For a split second, Griffin felt sucker punched.

Evie loving a man interested only in the hotel…

But history wasn't repeating itself. Despite the attraction between them, he had no reason to think Evie was actually falling for him. And he wasn't interested in the hotel, dammit! And just because his father was, that didn't mean Evelyn McClaren would sell to him.

Based on the murky history of whatever had happened the first time Evelyn hadn't sold to Frederick, Griffin had no reason to believe things would be different this time around. Especially not when he would do everything in his power to make sure this was one business deal his father failed to close.

Mentally grabbing hold of the throttle, he eased back on the emotions speeding through him. He still had this under control. Totally under control. "But what made you change your plan? You can't tell me that your aunt wouldn't let you buy into the hotel because of what your jerk of an ex almost did."

"No, but paying for the 'wedding that wasn't' had wiped out my savings." And Evie had had too much pride to allow her parents to foot the bill. "Then there were all the charge cards Eric had opened in my name and maxed out, destroying my credit and making it almost impossible for me to secure the business loan I would have needed at that point.

"So I went back to work where the partners offered me a raise if I were to stay and…I did. The longer I stayed in Portland and stayed away from Hillcrest House and even from my cousins, the harder it became to bridge that distance between us."

"But you came back, Evie. You were strong enough and brave enough—"

"Don't. Please." She shook her head, and the sheen of tears in her midnight eyes nearly brought him to his knees. "I'm none of those things. I came back because I was scared. Terrified, really."

"Of losing Hillcrest House?"

Evie shook her head. "Of losing my aunt. Last year she was diagnosed with breast cancer. She went through surgery, chemo, radiation treatments."

Griffin never would have guessed Evelyn McClaren was anything other than the picture of health. "She was lucky that the doctors caught it early enough for treatment."

He'd seen firsthand what happened when the dreaded disease was discovered too late. He'd watched how it had eaten away at his mother, leaving behind a shell of the woman she'd once been with no treatment, no cure, no hope in sight.

"She was lucky, and it was caught early, but not as

early as it could have been. My aunt was so busy running the hotel that she hadn't been taking care of herself. She wasn't keeping up with physicals and doctor's appointments, and if I'd been here—"

"Don't, Evie!" Griffin cut her off, grabbing her hand and squeezing hard, his heart breaking for the pain and worry written on her face. "Don't take that on yourself. Be thankful that your aunt has made a full recovery and that you have this second chance. Not everybody gets one."

He hadn't, but this wasn't about him or the chances he'd lost when he lost his mother. He didn't talk about his mother. Not ever.

They'd wandered quite a distance from the hotel along a flagstone path meandering through the grounds. They walked past the arched trellis that led to the rose garden, dormant now but waiting for the first hint of spring for the leaves to turn green and the fragrant blossoms to unfurl. As they rounded the bend, Griffin realized the path had led them straight to the gazebo adorned with twinkle lights and red and gold bows along the lattice fascia.

"I used to love it here," Evie said softly.

That was when Griffin knew. Where better to have a June wedding than at the elegant, airy gazebo nestled between the fragrant evergreens? Despite the overcast skies, the structure gleamed, its lacy scrollwork, intricate lattice and carved pillars brilliantly white against a verdant green backdrop.

"You must have a lot of good memories here."

"I did once." Her hand still in his, he felt her resistance, the tension telegraphing from the trembling of her slender fingers straight to his heart, but he stayed on the path toward the gazebo steps.

"Maybe it's time to make some new ones." He stopped

shy of the first stair, waiting for Evie to make that move. Either back toward the shadow of the past or forward into a brighter future.

"It's funny, you know," she said so softly he could barely hear the words. "How important a role this very spot has played in all our lives. Rory and Jamison fell in love here while making some repairs on the gazebo. And this is where Alexa told Chance she was pregnant."

New beginnings for her cousins at the very spot where her own dreams had ended. "You know what else it is?" At the slight shake of her head, he said, "This is the place where you kiss me for the very first time."

"We've already kissed. Or don't you remember?"

The bridal shop dressing room with mirrors on every side, a kaleidoscope of reflected images of Evie in his arms, her eyes dark with passion, her lips parted for his kiss… How could he not remember?

His voice rough with desire, Griffin promised, "I'll never forget. But *I* kissed *you*."

"I didn't realize we were keeping score."

Good thing, he thought vaguely as Evie set her slender foot on the first step. The added height brought her mouth level with his. As her lips brushed against his, any hope of playing by her rules fell by the wayside, and Griffin knew he was already lost.

Her fingers were cool against the heated skin at the back of his neck, and he burned even brighter when he imagined a more intimate touch. He wrapped an arm around her waist, bringing her body close to his on such a perfect level—her mouth even with his, the softness of her breasts at his chest, his hard arousal against the juncture of her thighs.

The last thing Griffin wanted to do was to take advantage when she was in an emotionally vulnerable state.

He tried keeping the kiss gentle, under control, but she was quick to remind him this was *her* kiss.

As her lips parted beneath his, all thoughts of control disappeared. He'd had a plane engine stall on him once, and that sensation of freefall was nothing compared to falling for Evie McClaren. But even as he let go, diving headlong into her kiss, her taste, her touch, Griffin couldn't help thinking that this time he was going to find out what it felt like to crash and burn.

Standing in the Primrose Suite the following afternoon, Evie studied the flower arrangement on the dining table with a critical eye. "What do you think? Is it perfect?" she asked Alexa as she adjusted the cut-glass vase. "It needs to be perfect."

"You do realize I am the bride, right?" her cousin's fiancée asked, a small smile on her beautiful face. "I should be the one obsessing over every detail."

"I'm not obsessing," Evie argued, ignoring the look the other woman shot her. She shifted the arrangement again and, recognizing she'd pretty much returned the thing back to its original position, she dropped her shoulders in a sigh. "Okay, so maybe I'm obsessing."

"As someone who's spent too much of her life striving for perfection, trust me when I tell you it's overrated."

Easy for Alexa to say. Even six months pregnant, the tall, elegant blonde didn't have a single hair out of place. Wearing a charcoal sweater dress that hugged her curves and the baby bump, which was the only weight she seemed to have gained, Alexa glanced around. "The room looks amazing, and it's not like my grandmother hasn't stayed here before."

"I know. But this is your wedding. This is special… It's important."

"Well, I certainly think so." Amusement filled the bride-to-be's voice.

"For Hillcrest House, I mean."

"Oh, of course." Though Alexa nodded solemnly, Evie realized she was still messing with the flowers. But instead of adjusting the arrangement this way and that, she'd plucked a pale pink rosebud from the mix and held the fragrant velvet-soft petals against her nose.

Clearing her throat, Evie stuck the stem back into the vase. "I'm glad we had this room available with your grandmother arriving a day earlier than expected."

Alexa rolled her eyes. "She'd insisted she wanted her chauffeur to drive her, but now she wants to fly. So thank goodness for Griffin."

"For Griffin?"

"Didn't he tell you?"

"He mentioned running some kind of prewedding errand today." Or, at least, Evie thought he'd said something of the sort.

She'd never intended to open up about Eric's betrayal the way she had yesterday. She liked to think she'd closed the door on a time in her life that made her feel stupidly foolish and naive. But she hadn't left the past behind at all—something Griffin had forced her to recognize.

In trying to slam the door to her past shut, she'd ended up trapping herself inside. When it came to taking that first step into the gazebo, the first step in truly facing Eric's betrayal, Griffin hadn't forced her at all. He'd simply stood by her side, encouraging her, waiting for her, believing in her.

The exhilarating rush of freedom had left her giddy and light-headed. Or maybe that had been the result of Griffin's kiss. Or was it *her* kiss since, as he'd pointed out, she was the one to kiss him?

But the moment her lips touched his, Evie hadn't cared who kissed who first or where one kiss ended and the next began. All she knew was that she never wanted to stop. And if Griffin had pressed, even a little, she would have been tempted to take him back to the cottage, where they could have made even more memories without the distraction of clothes getting in the way.

Instead, he had gradually and reluctantly pulled back. Or so she'd thought at the time. But when he'd made the comment about being busy with the upcoming wedding, Evie couldn't help but wonder if that hadn't been some kind of brush-off. Uncertainty had pushed its way to the forefront of her mind, crowding out the memories of the kiss with doubts and second thoughts.

At the sound of Alexa's grateful laugher, Evie turned her focus back to the conversation. "It's a bit more than an errand. Due to my grandmother's last-minute change of plans, she wasn't able to book her normal pilot and my grandmother can be…particular. Fortunately Griffin volunteered to pick her up. He isn't exactly leaping tall buildings in a single bound, but he is flying in to save the day. Or at least flying down to LA."

"He's… Oh, well. That is something, isn't it?" Evie had thought little of Griffin's ability. Flying planes had seemed to her like another way of flaunting the privileges that came with his family's wealth. Fast planes, fast cars, fast women…

Alexa's imperious eightysomething grandmother Virginia did not exactly make it into that category. And maybe, just maybe, the wealthy playboy role didn't fit Griffin as well as Evie thought it had a few days ago.

"Griffin's a good guy. One of the best."

Despite the lighthearted comment, Evie didn't miss Alexa's weighted sidelong glance. She could sense the other woman digging to see how deep Evie's feelings ran when she was unwilling to even scrape the surface.

"Alexa—"

"I know. I know. I'm sticking my nose where it doesn't belong. But Griffin's my best friend and has been for years, so that makes this my business, don't you think?"

"I think Griffin's probably dated plenty of women during all those years of friendship. His heart seems to have stayed very much intact."

"True, but don't fool yourself, Evie," Alexa advised gently. "Just because he keeps his heart well guarded, that doesn't mean it won't break. After all, aren't the most fragile things the ones we do our best to protect?"

As Evie spent the next hour preparing for Virginia Mayhew's arrival—making sure the chef had a list of specially requested meals, that they had her favorite tea on hand, that a car and driver would be available as needed—she told herself she didn't have time to think of her conversation with Alexa. She was far too busy to give a second thought to the absurd idea that Griffin James might be falling for her.

After all, they had a plan. One that came with a very specific set of rules. Rule number one: do not fall in love. Rule number two: do *not* fall in love. It was ridiculous to think that Griffin's heart was in any danger—least of all from her.

But when her phone sounded with his text later that afternoon, the skip in her heartbeat had little to do with the news that Alexa's grandmother had arrived.

Adjusting the hem of her short burgundy jacket and smoothing her hands down the matching skirt, Evie put on her most professional smile. As she stepped into the lobby, she took a moment to try to view the elegant entrance with a critical eye. The way a woman like Virginia Mayhew might.

Instead, Evie found herself noticing the Christmas decorations Rory kept adding—the red-and-white poinsettia floral arrangements on the concierge desk, a few ribbon-trimmed sprigs of mistletoe hanging from the walnut-paneled ceiling. As if they were drawn to the very air of romance, everywhere she looked, Evie saw couples matched up together. Checking in at the front desk, talking with the concierge, glancing through the brochures touting the Holly and Vine event that evening…

One pair in particular caught Evie's attention. She watched as Trisha stopped Aaron on his way back to the kitchen. The brief moment could have been nothing more than another argument over mushrooms, but Evie doubted it. Tension fairly sizzled between the two, and as Trisha tossed her head and met Aaron's scrutiny with a glare, Evie recognized a woman fighting her own attraction.

She should. The battle was one she was all too familiar with…and one she was close to losing.

Shaking off the thought, Evie turned her focus back to where it should have been and scanned the lobby again. As she finally spotted Alexa's grandmother, she couldn't help but smile. Not her professional, pasted-on smile, but a genuine tugged-straight-from-her-heartstrings smile.

With his arm supporting the austere octogenarian, Griffin slowed his typical take-charge stride to match her more careful steps. He bent his head to take a few inches off his impressive height and stoop closer to Virginia's level. Although he nodded in all seriousness at what looked to be a dressing-down by the older woman, Evie didn't miss the spark in his eyes. Not as he looked down at Alexa's grandmother and not when he glanced up and winked at Evie.

"Mrs. Mayhew." Striding over to greet the woman, Evie added, "Welcome back to Hillcrest House. We have our finest suite ready for you if you'd like to relax after your trip."

"I doubt I could possibly relax after that dreadful flight."

"Oh, come on, Mrs. M. I only took the plane into a death spiral twice, and you know you loved it."

"Griffin," Evie muttered in warning beneath her breath. After all the years of friendship between Griffin and Alexa, the elderly woman was no doubt familiar with his humor, but this wasn't the impression Evie wanted to make.

"Pay no attention to him, Ms. McClaren. He's been impossible ever since he was a young boy." Despite the woman's words, Evie saw a hint of fondness in Virginia Mayhew's faded blue eyes. "Now, if you would show me to my room, perhaps I will take a few moments to lie down after my near-death experience."

Undaunted, Griffin leaned in to kiss the woman's lined cheek. "As always, thank you for flying Griffin Air." Turning to Evie, he said, "I'll see you tonight." At her blank look, he added, "At Holly and Vine. From the sound of things, there's going to be quite a turnout. I'm sure everyone will be expecting us to go."

"Oh, right." Evie hadn't thought of asking Griffin to attend with her since she hadn't planned to make more than a five-minute appearance at the Hillcrest House booth. But Griffin was right. Between the shops staying open late on Main Street and the Christmas festival in the square, the whole town would be on hand. "I'll see you tonight."

As he brushed his lips against her cheek as well, he murmured, "And anytime you want me to show you the friendly skies, just say the word."

When she turned her attention away from Griffin's retreating figure, Virginia Mayhew was watching closely, an elegant eyebrow arched in disapproval.

"Right this way, Mrs. Mayhew." As Evie led the woman down the hallway to the Primrose Suite, she said, "We have you in the same suite as last time."

As they stepped inside, Virginia barely spared the room a glance before turning her somewhat intimidating focus back to Evie. "You should know that I wanted Alexa to get married at my estate. Southern California is beautiful this time of year."

Southern California was beautiful anytime of year; that was what made it Southern California. "We're all thrilled that she chose Hillcrest House. And considering your granddaughter is marrying the wedding coordinator's brother, I assure you the ceremony has been planned down to the tiniest detail."

"With such an important event, I would hate to think your attention might be split due to certain…distractions."

Perfect. What was it about the Primrose Suite that made Mayhew women think they needed to offer advice on Evie's relationship with Griffin? "Mrs. Mayhew—"

"You should know Griffin has never been the settling-down type. I've seen how women throw themselves at him. After all, he's handsome, charming…rich. But Griffin isn't a man to get serious about. Not when he isn't serious about anything."

Evie sucked in a deep breath, trying to cool the heat rising inside her. It shouldn't have bothered her as much as it did. Not after the older woman's careless dismissal of Hillcrest House. Not when Virginia had lumped Evie in with the scores of women who would shamelessly chase after the wealthy, eligible bachelor.

It shouldn't have been Virginia Mayhew's criticism of Griffin that had Evie fighting to hold on to her temper. After all, she'd accused him of the very same thing. But wasn't she also starting to realize she'd misjudged him?

"Griffin does like to joke around."

Just because he keeps his heart well guarded, that doesn't mean it won't break.

Was Alexa right? Was Griffin's outwardly carefree attitude some kind of defense mechanism? Not a superficial response because he didn't care, but a carefully thought-out deflection to keep people from learning he cared too deeply?

"But that doesn't mean he isn't serious when it comes to the people close to him. People like Alexa. I doubt there's anything he wouldn't do for her." Meeting Virginia's eyes, Evie added, "Like making an unexpected round-trip flight so that her grandmother is in the front row when Alexa says 'I do.'"

Chapter Ten

Downtown Clearville had pulled out all the stops for the first annual Holly and Vine event. The shops along Main Street sported green, red and white awnings over every door, and the windows were decorated with wreaths and silver bells. Every tree along either side of the street was wrapped in hundreds of twinkling lights, and silver stars and snowflake ornaments glittered in the branches. Christmas carols and laughter surrounded Evie as she made her way toward the town square. Everywhere she turned, couples strolled hand in hand. The very air around her smelled like hot cocoa and roasted, cinnamon-sugar-coated nuts.

"Sweets for a sweet." Sliding a hand around her waist, Griffin held out a star-shaped chocolate lollipop.

"No one thinks I'm sweet," Evie protested, though she couldn't resist a smile as she accepted the treat and bit off a corner.

"Maybe no one's kissed you like I have."

There was no *maybe* about it. No one kissed her, teased her, annoyed her, emboldened her, the way Griffin did. Holding up the lollipop for him, Evie said, "I'm pretty sure last time *I* kissed *you*."

The flirtatious challenge coming from her lips sounded nothing like her, but Evie wasn't surprised. She didn't feel like the same person. At least, not like the same person she'd been since her broken engagement. Being with Griffin, telling him about Eric when she hadn't even told her family or friends the real reason behind the breakup, had freed something inside her.

Eric was the one who'd been in the wrong, and it was past time she stopped blaming herself. She'd never set out to bury herself in work as some kind of penance or punishment. At first, she'd focused on building her savings back up after paying her parents back for the nonwedding, as if erasing the deficit in her bank account would somehow erase the hole in her heart.

But her aunt was right. She'd allowed her professional life to take over. Her career had become her refuge and her excuse—for not having fun, for not having time for friends and family...

The fourth F in her plan—*falling in love*—hovered around her, floating on the edges of her subconscious like the star-shaped ornaments gleaming in her peripheral vision. Almost close enough for her to reach out and grab the elusive promise of a wish come true, but far enough away that she could turn ever so slightly and lose sight of it altogether.

It isn't real, Evie reminded herself, despite the pressure in her chest that made it feel as if her heart was expanding, pushing the boundaries and coming dangerously close to bursting.

But maybe she wanted it to be real. Just for a little while. Like the twinkle lights and the decorations. Something she could enjoy for the moment, even though she knew it could never last.

Griffin wrapped his fingers around her wrist. Her too-full heart pounded like crazy as he lifted the decadent treat to his mouth and savored the bite. When he closed his lips around her thumb and licked a small smear from her skin, it was all Evie could do not to melt like the chocolate on his tongue.

"Griffin." His name caught in her dry throat, her pulse pounding in her ears so loudly she could barely hear the sound of her own voice or the familiar chime of...

Wedding bells?

"I, um, that's Rory." She'd programmed in the ringtone for her cousin as a joke, but it was hard to remember she was too smart, too focused, too logical to fall in love, when Griffin James could make her forget everything with a look, a touch, a kiss...

Maybe it's time to make some new memories.

And maybe forgetting wasn't such a bad thing after all.

"For someone who makes her living bringing couples together, your cousin could have better timing," Griffin said wryly. But he gave her hand a final squeeze and stepped back, allowing them both to take a much-needed breath.

With her skin still tingling from his kiss, Evie reached into her purse for her cell. "Hey, Rory." She cringed at the overly bright sound of her voice and tried to tone it down as she asked, "How's everything going?"

"It's been great so far and the booth is—well, it's amazing. Jamison really outdid himself, but I got a call from the babysitter who is watching Hannah. Her grandmother's been taken to the hospital. I'd try to find another sitter, but everyone's already busy. I don't suppose you could take over the booth for the rest of the night?"

Typically Rory and Trisha handled promotions for the hotel. Both women excelled at engaging potential guests face-to-face, allowing Evie to disappear into the woodwork of her small office.

But she hated the idea of not pulling her own weight and with this emergency situation, she immediately said, "I'm already here and will head that way now."

"Thanks for this, Evie. I really appreciate it. And, well, about the booth. I should probably tell you…"

"You can fill me in when I get there," Evie reassured her cousin. "I'll be over in a minute."

"Everything okay?" Griffin asked as he walked back over after throwing the lollipop stick away in a nearby trash can.

Evie had never had a problem putting work first, but she couldn't deny her disappointment as she gave a quick explanation and said, "Sorry to have to cut the night short."

"Who says we have to?"

"Oh, come on. You don't want to hang out at a booth, handing out Hillcrest House brochures the rest of the night."

"Maybe I want to hang out with you whatever you're doing." Before she could offer another protest, he said, "I'll grab us something to drink and meet you over there."

Watching Griffin walk away, Evie couldn't make her own feet move. A group of women heading in the opposite direction slowed, heedless of holding up the foot traffic behind them, to check him out. Evie couldn't blame them. He was easily the most breathtaking man she'd ever seen. She also couldn't stop the possessive feeling of pride that, for now at least, he was hers.

Something Griffin seemed to confirm when he glanced back, as if knowing all along she'd still be waiting, still be watching. He flashed a sexy smile and a wink over his shoulder.

Shaking her head at her own foolishness, Evie hurried off toward the square only to do some traffic stopping of her own. The heart of downtown was a winter wonderland of red and green booths, tables draped with bright bunting and thousands of twinkle lights glittering in the trees. She didn't have to look too closely or try to guess which of the stands belonged to Hillcrest House. There, front and center, amid the typical and somewhat boring pop-up tents and shade structures, was a perfect miniature replica of Hillcrest's own gazebo, decked out with garlands and mistletoe and Christmas lights.

Standing on the front steps, Rory caught sight of Evie and offered a quick wave before rushing over. "Jamison did this. Can you believe it?" she asked, referring to her fiancé. "When he told me he wanted to work on a booth for the event, I had no idea he was going to do something like this. He wanted it to be a surprise, so surprise!"

Rory's smile faded, though, as she added, "I'm sorry, Evie—"

"Why?" Evie quickly cut off the apology. "This is— amazing. And I'm guessing Hannah is thrilled to have a new playhouse."

Rory nodded. "She can't wait for Jamison to reassemble it in the backyard. She'd already promised to invite all her stuffed animals to a tea party." Worrying her lower lip between her teeth, she said, "I wanted to warn you…"

"Warn me? Good grief, Rory, it's a tiny gazebo, not a haunted mansion." A place where a four-year-old would soon be serving imaginary tea. If that wasn't enough to dispel Evie's ghosts, then she could think of one thing that would.

I kissed Griffin James for the first time on the steps of Hillcrest's gazebo.

But it was more than that. More than a kiss. It was the step she'd taken into the present, maybe even a step toward the future. Eric's betrayal and her feelings of guilt and blame were part of the past. By encouraging her to take that step, to take that kiss, Griffin had shown her how to take control. A new memory could go a long way toward erasing an old one.

"You're sure you're okay with this? I mean, I honestly didn't think you'd even set foot in the gazebo after you broke up with Eric."

Rory would have been right…right up until the day before. But it was still with a sense of accomplishment that Evie said, "Well, you're wrong. I have a lot of good memories about that gazebo." Mostly old, but some new enough to make her cheeks heat under her cousin's watchful eye.

Turning her attention to the booth, Evie reached out and trailed her hand over the carved railing. "And this is amazing." Despite the sting of tears at the back of her throat, she turned to her cousin with a smile. "It's like Jamison is announcing to everyone who sees it how much he loves you."

"Oh, Evie." Her cousin blinked back tears of her own. "That's such a beautiful thing to say. And I'm so…glad that you can be happy for us."

"You and Jamison are perfect for each other." Before either of them could really start crying, she added, "And what can I say? It must be the Christmas spirit bringing out the best in me."

Rory laughed. "I think someone other than jolly Saint

Nick might be responsible." She tilted her head, and Evie glanced over her shoulder in time to see Griffin approach with two steaming mugs.

"Thought you could use something to warm you up." Flashing a wink, he added, "And I brought hot chocolate, too."

"Griffin." Rory greeted him with a friendlier smile than Evie might have expected as she accepted the warm mug and breathed in the chocolate-scented steam.

"How has the turnout been so far?" he asked.

"It's been amazing," her cousin gushed. "I'm sure this is going to be a yearly event from now on. I've booked five appointments for couples who want to tour Hillcrest House and we already have fifty people signed up for our newsletter. Fifty more and we'll hit our goal!"

The goal had been Evie's idea and had seemed doable at the time, but now that she was the one tasked with getting those final names, she wished she'd aimed a little lower.

"What do you think, Evie?" Griffin asked. "Maybe we should sign up for that tour."

Rory's jaw dropped. Evie couldn't bring herself to look at Griffin, but he didn't let that stop him. He pressed a kiss against her temple, and her body instantly turned toward his. And while she knew she shouldn't, with her cousin staring at them, her eyes as wide as brilliant blue spotlights, Evie couldn't resist saying, "I hardly think there's reason for a tour. You know I'd never get married anywhere other than Hillcrest."

"Then there you have it," Griffin murmured in agreement. "Hillcrest House it is."

By the end of the evening, both the number of email addresses and the couples signed up to tour the hotel as a potential wedding venue had far exceeded Evie's quotas. It was all thanks to Griffin. Not that that was any surprise. People—and not just women—loved him.

For Evie, speaking with strangers, even making small talk, often made her feel self-conscious and awkward and far too likely to say the wrong thing. But every time she tried to ease away, Griffin pulled her back to the center of the conversation. He encouraged her to discuss the hotel's past with a man who was a retired history professor. To talk about the rose garden with the woman who boasted an I Heart Flowers pin on her floral denim jacket. To inform couples who wanted their wedding to take place outdoors when the grounds and weather were at their best. To promise longed-for solitude during the off-season to a man looking for a secluded retreat to finish his first novel.

And instead of simply taking one of their brochures with half-hearted interest, more and more people had stayed longer, asking questions, signing up for the mailing list and even using the gazebo as a backdrop for photographs.

The energy and excitement surrounding the event created more of a buzz inside Evie than if she'd visited every wine tasting booth in the square. And the way Griffin looked at her—a combination of pleasure and pride—had her head spinning in a way that no fruit of the vine ever could.

"So, is it true?" a young woman asked before glancing at the man by her side with a teasing smile. "Is Hillcrest House really magic?"

Evie's heart sank a little at the woman's excitement and expectation. Tailoring facts and figures to suit a potential guest's interest was one thing. Weaving tales about magic and the promise of happily-ever-after, that was something else. "Hillcrest House is a gorgeous place for a wedding," she said, gesturing toward the tablet and the streaming slideshow set up on the sign-up table. "My cousin Rory is the wedding coordinator, and the work she does is—" *do not say* magic, *do not say* magic, *do not say* magic "—remarkable," she finished.

The brunette's face fell ever so slightly, and Evie rushed to try and recapture her interest. She held out the clipboard and pen. "If you'd like to sign up, my cousin can arrange a tour for you."

Stepping closer to Evie's side, Griffin wrapped an arm around her waist. "This is an amazing replica, but it's nothing compared to the real gazebo. It's a special place to us, isn't it, sweetheart?"

"It is," she admitted, not having to embellish the truth at all. The warmth in his smile was all the encouragement she needed to add, "It's where I kissed you for the first time."

"And Hillcrest House is where we met."

"I knew it!" the woman practically crowed. "I knew it was magic."

"That is something you'll have to see for yourself," Griffin advised, half challenging, half teasing as he tapped the pen on the clipboard before handing it to the couple to add their names to the growing list.

"You know, you didn't have to stay the whole time," Evie said at the end of the night. Jamison had arranged for the gazebo to be taken down in the morning, so as the clock struck nine, Evie and Griffin were free to go.

"I wouldn't have missed it because then I would have missed this."

"Missed—"

Griffin pointed toward a stage at the center of the

square as the lead singer repeated, "Sorry, folks, this is our curtain call. Find someone special for the last dance."

Griffin held out his hand, and as the opening strains of a rock ballad filled the night air, she couldn't resist sliding her palm into his. She balked, but only for a brief second, as he led her up the gazebo steps. *No ghosts*, she reminded herself. Not tonight.

Evie had never been one to feel the need to fill a silence with inane conversation, but she needed some kind of distraction from the crazy pounding going on inside her chest. Maybe if she opened her mouth to talk, she'd remember how to breathe, because at the moment she felt light-headed enough to wonder if she wasn't about to pass out...

"You were amazing," she said. "With the booth and all, I mean."

"I was thinking the same thing about you. You know everything about Hillcrest House from the ground up."

"Most people usually aren't all that interested."

"Once people see how passionate you are, they're more likely to take an interest."

Evie didn't think her passions were something she should be thinking about, not when Griffin was holding her close, their bodies swaying in time with the music.

"Still...I suppose it's a good thing we'll have a lawyer in the family soon," she said.

Griffin's lips quirked in a bemused grin. "Why is that?"

"With all your talk about the hotel's magic, we'll be lucky if we don't get sued for false advertising when our guests fail to find elves or fairies or whatever it is they're hoping for."

"I'm pretty sure you're safe. People who believe in

magic will always find it. The ones who don't will never bother to look."

His words made perfect sense. Magic wasn't real. It was a simple matter of people seeing what they wanted to see. So why did the idea of never finding magic still seem so...sad?

"Evie." She looked up at his husky murmur. The awareness, the understanding in his expression, had a part of her wanting to run away as fast as she could. Another part of her never wanted to leave the certainty of the strong arms wrapped around her. "Close your eyes," he urged.

At her questioning glance, he added, "Some things don't have to be seen to be believed. Some things you just have to feel."

Evie's eyelids drifted shut the moment his lips touched hers. His mouth swallowed her quick gasp, stealing the oxygen from her lungs, but who needed air when there was this? When there was music and laughter and dancing beneath the stars?

It was amazing. It was incredible. It was...magic.

Chapter Eleven

Hours later, Evie lay in bed, wide-awake and staring up at the darkened ceiling.

Close your eyes.

Griffin's murmur whispered through her thoughts, but total darkness made the memories that much more potent and she was once again in Griffin's arms. She could hear that husky voice in her ear, breathe in the spicy, masculine scent of his cologne, feel the warmth of his hand at her waist, the brush of his thighs against her own…

Her frustrated cry seemed to echo in the silence of her bedroom as she kicked off the covers. Maybe a midnight snack would help. She didn't need to raid the cottage's tiny kitchen to know her own refrigerator was practically empty. She ate most of her meals at her desk, courtesy of the hotel's dining room. And other than giving in to Griffin's offer of chocolate, she'd resisted temptation at the festival.

And how long do you think that will last? a mocking voice taunted as she pulled on a pair of leggings. She wasn't worried about the temptation of sinfully sweet desserts but rather the temptation of sinfully seductive Griffin James...

She pulled a tunic-length navy sweater over her head and glanced in the mirror above the vanity. Her hair was too short to suffer a serious case of bed head, but she had washed all traces of makeup off when she came home.

No foundation, no eyeliner, no mascara, no lipstick... yet that didn't stop her lips from being a rosy pink, almost as if they, too, were clinging to the memory of Griffin's kiss.

Swallowing a curse, Evie hit the light switch and plunged the bathroom into darkness. She wasn't going to run into Griffin. She'd go the back way into the hotel kitchen with no one the wiser. Slipping out of the small cottage, Evie burrowed into her sweater and made her way down the path. The night air was cold and silent, carrying the distant hint of a burning fireplace. Though the lights glowed in welcome from the porch and front lobby, Evie circled the wraparound porch toward the rear entrance.

Evie pulled her key out and unlocked the back door. She stepped inside the kitchen and hit the lights only to jump a foot at the sound of a startled scream.

It took her pupils a moment to adjust before she wished they hadn't. Trisha and Aaron were locked together in a heated embrace with the redhead sitting on one of the stainless steel industrial counters, her legs locked around the handsome chef's waist.

"Oh, my—Evie, I am—we're so sorry." Trisha scrambled out of Aaron's embrace, giving the man a glare when he mumbled something that sounded a lot like "Not that sorry."

Snapping her jaw shut, Evie blinked a few times. She was relieved to see that, other than a few loosened buttons and an untucked shirt, both Trisha and Aaron were fully clothed. "I was coming down for a midnight snack. I guess that's what brought the two of you down here, as well." Only Evie had had a bowl of ice cream in mind.

"Aaron, um, was letting me try his risotto before we, um, add it to the menu for the New Year's Eve Ball." Trisha's face was nearly as red as her hair as she sneaked a glance at the man by her side.

"I take it you like mushrooms after all?" Evie asked wryly.

"Right? I mean, who knew?"

Evie had. Or at least she'd suspected the bickering couple had been fighting over something other than black truffles.

"We didn't plan for anything like this to happen," Trisha confessed, misery and maybe a hint of shock filling her voice. "It's so totally unprofessional. We *work* here. And in the kitchen of all places!"

The poor woman looked so horrified, Evie couldn't help but reassure her. "I don't think kissing will lead to too many major health violations."

"So you're not mad?"

Maybe she should have been. After all, Trisha and Aaron were employees, and making out on hotel grounds was pretty far from appropriate behavior. But what if she had run into Griffin along the shadowy, moon-kissed path leading to the hotel? If he'd pulled her into his arms, even in full view of the towering Victorian, did she really think she would have had the strength to resist?

Evie knew she had a reputation at the hotel as an ice

queen, no-nonsense and no fun, but she wasn't a hypocrite. "You're both mature, responsible adults. What you do on your own time is your own business."

The tension in Trisha's shoulders fell away. "You know how important Hillcrest is to me. And I promise you I would never let this relationship interfere with work."

Conviction rang in the other woman's voice, but Evie knew it was one promise she might not be able to keep. Trisha and Aaron's working relationship was bound to change if their personal relationship went up in flames.

But what if it doesn't? Griffin's voice whispered in her ear.

As Aaron stepped up beside Trisha, taking her hand, the two of them presenting a united front, Evie thought maybe they had a chance of making love last. Maybe someday, if she were willing to take that chance, she would, too.

The next morning, following his run on the beach, Griffin phoned the assistant project manager to get an update on the hotel in Dubai.

"I hear congratulations are in order!"

As Kevin Montoya's excited voice came across the line, for a split second, Griffin thought of Evie and their teasing banter the night before. The playful implication that their relationship had progressed to a point where they were discussing marriage.

From the moment he'd taken Evie's hand and led her toward the gazebo, visions of standing in that same spot, waiting while she walked toward him, her slender frame draped in white, had teased him. Only Griffin wasn't laughing.

Still, neither the thoughts in his head nor the Clearville grapevine could have reached halfway across the world. "Congratulations for what?"

"I heard your dad pulled off the deal in Tokyo. Sounds like you'll be heading to Japan!"

Excitement lifted the younger man's voice an octave, but Griffin's own response barely registered above a low murmur. "Great."

"You know," Kevin said, clearing his throat, "I was wondering if maybe I could assist on that project. The hotel here will be up and running by then, and I mean, Japan!" So much excitement thrummed in the other man's words, Griffin was surprised the cell phone wasn't vibrating in his hand. "That is, if you were happy with the job I did here."

The hotel in Dubai had been Griffin's first time working with Kevin, and the kid had done an amazing job. He'd taken every roadblock as an exciting challenge to be conquered, and he'd risen above each time. "I guess we can both make that sake toast tonight."

"Seriously? This going to be so awesome! Thanks, Griffin!"

"Don't thank me. You earned it. You've worked hard, Kevin."

After spending the next few minutes going over the details, Griffin ended the call and tossed the phone onto the suite's floral couch when what he really wanted to do was chuck it into the ocean.

Japan.

His gut clenched at the thought of spending another year or two of his life overseas and away from home.

Home. That was a joke.

The mansion where he'd grown up had stopped feeling like a home after his mother died. As far as his father was concerned, home was wherever a James hotel was.

But for Griffin, just because his name was on the sign, that didn't make it home.

Just because he was the heir to the empire, that didn't make James Hotels his dream, either. It was his father's. Despite all the years he'd tried to put in the effort, to focus on the work, to take pride in all he'd accomplished, Griffin had to face that he would never be happy following in Frederick's footsteps. Not when each step he took in that direction seemed to cement him more firmly to the ground, when all he wanted was to be in the air.

But how was he supposed to quit the family business without quitting the family? Without quitting his father?

As the walls closed in on him, Griffin knew of only one thing that would set him free. He needed to fly. This was the first time, however, that he didn't want to be flying solo.

Evie blinked at the computer screen, but the numbers seemed to blur and dance as she tried to reconcile a stack of vendor invoices. If there was anything that normally gave her a sense of satisfaction, it was the logic and certainty of numbers. When it came to accounting, one plus one always equaled two.

But reconciling the $225.37 discrepancy couldn't hold her attention as it usually would. She leaned back in her chair, wincing as her spine gave a series of loud sequential pops. She was tired, that was all. Between the holiday rush, the wedding in two days, and the New Year's Eve Ball the following week, she was burning the candle at both ends. Add in a sleepless night, and no wonder she was exhausted.

And yet…her schedule, demanding as it was, hadn't really changed much in the past months. She'd been pushing to prove herself ever since Evelyn had handed over the reins in her absence.

So why did Evie feel like something was…missing? Some spark, some excitement, something…more. Something that made her want to turn off her computer, escape the isolation of her office and—find Griffin.

"Get a grip, Evie," she muttered to herself as she grabbed her coffee cup and winced at the taste of the cold, bitter brew. "You have a job to do."

She didn't need Griffin James in her life. She didn't need his laughter or his sexy smiles or the way he made her feel as if he'd uncorked a bottle of champagne inside her and she could float around on a cloud of fizzy bubbles.

She was too smart, too serious, too focused to need any of that.

But, oh, how she wanted it!

Evie didn't have to look at her calendar app to know their time was running out. She sucked in a sharp breath that did little to ease the pressure building inside her chest. She was going to miss him. The endless days stretched out in front of her and she could scroll through month after month after month with nothing but Hillcrest House events in sight.

But wasn't that what she wanted? Wasn't the hotel *all* she wanted and the only reason she'd started the charade of dating Griffin in the first place?

"Evie?"

She jumped at the sound of her aunt's voice, startled to realize Evelyn had stepped into the office without her noticing. "Aunt E, good morning. How are you?"

"I'm fine. But how are *you* this morning?"

"I'm fine. Last night was…" Her voice trailed off, unable to come up with a fitting description. She'd gone from almost dreading the Holly and Vine event to enjoying herself more than she could have imagined. Even filling in for Rory had been a huge success—thanks to Griffin.

"Ah, yes, I heard about last night. Rory called me first thing this morning. She mentioned you might have some exciting news to share."

News? Evie tried to focus on the number of couples who had signed up for tours or the email addresses they had gathered for the hotel's newsletter, but like with the inventory, the facts and figures normally so easily within her grasp eluded her. "I, um…"

She reached for her tablet, but her aunt beat her to it. Perched on the edge of the desk, Aunt E placed a hand over the closed cover. "About you and Griffin?" Her aunt practically glowed. "Getting married right here at Hillcrest House?"

"Married!" Evie shot to her feet as if launched from her chair.

"Has he already proposed?"

"What? No!"

"But you think he's going to, right?" her aunt pressed.

"Why…" Evie's voice trailed away as she realized exactly why her aunt thought she and Griffin were getting engaged. All because of what they'd said the night before.

I'd never get married anywhere other than Hillcrest. Then there you have it. Hillcrest House it is.

But they'd been *joking.* And while Evie certainly knew better than to take Griffin's words seriously, Rory did not.

No, her cousin, with her fairy-tale belief in happily-ever-after, would grab hold of any hint of another McClaren wedding in the future. Even one as preposterous as Evie McClaren to Griffin James…

"You talked to Rory," Evie repeated.

"I did, but it's not like I—like all of Clearville—

couldn't see for myself." At Evie's confused look, her aunt lifted the tablet and called up a familiar website—one that documented local events. And there, right beneath the headline touting the success of Holly and Vine, was a photo of Evie and Griffin kissing in the middle of the gazebo—for all of Clearville to see.

Evie hadn't noticed anyone taking a picture. But what was a camera flash compared to the very stars exploding inside her whenever she and Griffin kissed?

Looking at the image, Evie couldn't blame her aunt or cousin for believing what they were seeing. Because for a pretend couple, the emotion, the passion captured in that one photo looked very, very real indeed...

"This is so wonderful, Evie! It's the best Christmas present ever! I'm so happy for you and so proud."

Proud? Despite the excitement written on her aunt's face, the last thing Evie was feeling was proud. If she had a word to describe the overwhelming, dizzying emotion spinning through her brain, it would be closer to *panic*. Dating was one thing. People casually dated all the time.

But an engagement? That was serious. That was a commitment. That was...a short walk down the aisle away from *marriage*!

"I've been worried about you. Ever since Eric... Well, I saw how you closed off your heart and how work took over your entire life. We're so alike, you and I, and I've been so afraid of you making the same mistake I did. But seeing you with Griffin... It's made me realize that we're not so alike after all."

"But, Aunt E—"

"You've been brave enough to give love a second chance. When it comes to having a career and following your heart, Evie, you've found a way to have both."

Hillcrest House and a life.

That had been her plan all along, hadn't it? A goal that finally, *finally* seemed within reach. All thanks to her pretend boyfriend turning into her pretend fiancé.

Griffin headed down the hallway toward the lobby. He skirted around couples and young families heading to the dining room for the continental breakfast or out to do some holiday sightseeing.

Griffin's anticipation grew with every step he took. He had everything arranged. Now all he needed was to get Evie to say yes. After the way she'd opened up about the past the day before, after the kisses they'd shared, he wouldn't be surprised if she wanted to slow things down. To take a step back…

"Griffin!"

He'd barely set foot inside the lobby when he heard Evelyn McClaren call out his name. As she and Evie walked out of Evie's office, tucked in behind the concierge's desk, a bright smile lit the older woman's face and she greeted him with an exuberant wave.

Evie's expression was somewhat less welcoming, but as far as taking a step back went? That wasn't happening. After saying something to her aunt, Evie made a beeline straight for him. Tucking a lock of hair behind one ear, she seemed to take a deep breath as she headed his way.

Her narrow pin-striped skirt and sapphire silk blouse were strictly professional, but Griffin saw signs of the real woman beneath in the color highlighting her cheeks and the hands clasped nervously at her slender waist.

"Morning, sweetheart."

"Griffin, we need to talk." Casting a glance over her shoulder at her aunt, Evie stuttered, "I—we—" As she tried without success to get the words out, Griffin took advantage. Leaning close, he brushed a kiss against her parted lips.

He'd meant nothing more than a light touch, but the fires banked the night before needed only a single spark. She tasted as sweet as the chocolate they'd shared under the stars, and it took everything inside him not to pull her into his arms and kiss her for real.

For real...

As if anything he was doing, as if anything he'd done since setting foot in Clearville, hadn't been 100 percent genuine.

Almost as if reading his thoughts, Evie said, "I thought you didn't want to kiss me for show."

"That wasn't for show, Evie. That was for me."

After staring at him for a moment, she shook her head and muttered, "Just remember, this is all your fault."

"Well, that's no surprise. But what exactly am I to blame for this time?"

"After last night, my cousin and aunt think we're practically engaged."

"Engaged?" Even as the word seemed to echo through the lobby, even as Evie sternly shushed him, images rebounded through his brain. Kissing Evie at the gazebo, the very spot where she'd once dreamed of saying "I do," the unspoken loss and longing when she'd stared at the wedding dress at the shop in town. And then memory and imagination collided until Evie was wearing the wedding dress, walking toward the gazebo where he waited...

"Evie..."

"I know! It's crazy, right?" She filled him in on Rory's call to her aunt and the evidently infamous photo. Then she added, "But what was I supposed to say when she told me how proud she was of me? How could I tell her that none of it was real?"

And just like that, the images disappeared.

Not real.

Evie had impeccable timing. He'd give her that. Just when he was on the edge of forgetting, leave it to her to remind him.

"My aunt wouldn't come right out and say so, but I know she's having second thoughts about selling the hotel. It's a lot to ask, but we're already pretending to date. Is it really that much more of a stretch to pretend we're in love? And it's only for a little longer."

Pretend he was in love with Evie for a few more days? If Griffin wasn't careful, he'd spend the rest of his life pretending he wasn't.

Taking refuge behind the comfort of a carefree smile, he said, "Leave it to you to overachieve. You wanted a boyfriend to prove to your aunt that you have a life, but hey, now you can add another F to your plan. What was it again? Friends, family, fun...and now a fiancé."

"Something like that," Evie murmured. "So...you're okay with this?"

"It so happens I already have some experience in the pretend-fiancé department." He'd been 100 percent sincere when he'd proposed to Alexa, thinking at the time that friendship could make for a successful marriage. That the caring, the lasting, if platonic, love he had for her was as strong as any emotion he could ever feel. It was little wonder Alexa had been reluctant to say yes.

He'd been a complete fool.

"But what about what happens later? I realize it's not how you and I handle things, but most people actually get married after getting engaged."

"We'll still stick with the plan. After the New Year's Eve Ball, we'll keep up the charade of a long-distance relationship. Once Rory and I have convinced my aunt not to sell, we'll announce that the relationship didn't work out."

"Just like that?"

Evie nodded, but he couldn't help noticing the small movement wasn't quite as decisive as her words. "Just like that," she whispered.

Thinking of the arrangements he'd made, of the day he'd planned for the two of them, Griffin knew he should be the one taking a step back. But like the fool he was, he was going to keep rushing blindly toward the heartbreak dead ahead. "All right, then, but first we need to celebrate."

"Celebrate?"

"Well, we did just get engaged, didn't we? And how better to do that than to sneak away from work for a romantic rendezvous?"

Chapter Twelve

Evie said yes.

She still couldn't believe she'd said yes to a romantic rendezvous with Griffin James. And not because her aunt wanted her to go out and have fun. To pursue a life outside work. No, Evie hadn't said yes because of what her aunt wanted for her.

She'd said yes because she wanted this, because she wanted Griffin, all for herself.

Even if he was driving her crazy at the moment.

"You're not going to tell me where we're going?" she demanded, and not for the first time, as he guided his rental car down the winding road leading out of town.

"I told you we're going for a ride."

She waved toward the windshield, where a view of the towering redwoods passed by in an evergreen blur. "But a ride where?"

"You'll see" was all Griffin would say.

"Should I mention that I'm not one for surprises?" Evie asked as the miles flew by and Griffin's smug know-it-all silence made it clear he wasn't going to tell her anything.

"Should I mention that's completely obvious?"

She opened her mouth to argue, but what could she possibly say? Her copious notes and lists, her religious updating of her calendar to track every appointment, every event, her constant checking of her email, none of it was about staying organized as much as it was about staying in control.

As if reading her mind, Griffin reached over and took her hand. He unfolded her fingers, which were curled into a fist, and linked them with his own. "You can trust me, Evie. Just let go," he encouraged her, "and enjoy the ride."

The unspoken reminder that this whole wild ride would be over soon echoed in the confines of the car. Did it really matter where they were going or what they were doing? Did anything matter other than spending what time they had together?

"I'll try," she said with a put-upon sigh, "if you'll do me one favor."

"And what is that?"

Dropping the attitude in favor of an honesty and sincerity that came straight from her heart, Evie asked, "Can you make it last?"

"That was incredible!"

The last place Evie had expected they might end up was the small regional airport outside the nearby town of Redfield. Even though Griffin had promised her a ride, the words still hadn't quite registered until she found herself on the tarmac surrounded by private planes. "I mean, I knew you were a pilot, but that—that was amazing!"

Her feet were back on solid ground, but she still felt as

though she were soaring. Sitting beside Griffin as they flew along the rugged, rocky coastline, she'd seen more than the gorgeous view outside the cockpit window. She'd felt as if she were seeing the real Griffin. Not the cocky, impetuous, joking version he showed to the rest of the world, but a confident, controlled, serious version hiding behind the sexy smile. A sexy smile she had full opportunity to witness as she added, "You were amazing!"

Evie expected some kind of witty sexual innuendo after the way she'd left herself open with that effusive compliment, but instead, Griffin said, "Flying is something that I… Well, it's something I love. And I'm glad I could share it with you."

Something he loved…

The sincerity in Griffin's deep voice made her pulse pound in a way no sexy, teasing comment ever could have. Sucking in a deep breath, she dragged her attention away from him to take a look around. On their approach, the airfield had looked like nothing more than a narrow strip carved out of the wilderness with a dense forest on one side and a sheer cliff that dropped off into the ocean on the other.

From the ground, the area looked even more isolated, with the tall evergreens standing guard on one side and the sea and sky blending into blues and grays on the distant horizon. "Where are we?"

Griffin chuckled at the awe underlying the words. "At a private airstrip about an hour's drive outside Clearville. We took the scenic route to get here."

They certainly had, and Evie had surprised herself by enjoying every second. She'd done exactly as Griffin had asked. She'd trusted him and let go.

"How did you—you know what? Forget I asked." She didn't want to know how he'd discovered the out-of-the-way location or what he'd had to pay to convince the owner to allow him to land there.

"Are you ready for your surprise?"

Evie blinked in response. "Seriously? There's more?"

"Seriously," Griffin answered with a grin. "There's more."

Taking her hand, he led her toward the rugged cliff overlooking the ocean. "Watch your step," he advised.

Her step? Evie was pretty sure her next step was going to be about thirty feet straight down. But as she reached the edge, she saw the rough-hewn stairs carved into the side of the windswept cliff and a twisted metal railing following the crisscrossing path all the way down to a narrow strip of beach. "Ready?" Griffin asked.

Standing on the edge of the rocky precipice, her heart was pounding, but Evie knew her reaction had little to do with the intimidating descent ahead of her. As she placed her hand in Griffin's, feeling the warmth, the strength, the—heaven help her—promise in his confident grip, she couldn't help the laugh that bubbled out of her.

"What's so funny?" he asked as he led the way down the craggy steps.

"I should be reconciling inventory right now."

"Well, that does sound far more interesting."

"No, actually, it doesn't." Not even for someone like her, who lived for balancing accounts, reconciling inventory and forecasting budgets. But that was real life. Private planes? Romantic beaches where it was easy to believe they were the only two people on earth? That wasn't… Well, it certainly wasn't a typical Thursday, that was for sure.

No, this was more like, well, Christmas. A special gift, set apart from the day-in, day-out reality of living. A moment out of time and one to be treasured before the calendar turned to a day, a week, a month after month after month with no chance of anything so romantic or exciting in her future.

Evie kept a grip on the cold metal railing as they made their way down the cliff face, but it was Griffin's warm hand in hers that gave her the greatest sense of security. He wouldn't he let her fall.

As her sensible heels sank into the soft sand, Evie gasped as she realized the surprises truly had yet to end. In a small, sheltered cove carved into the rock and protected from the wind blowing off the ocean, a red-and-green-checked blanket was spread out, held in place by a large wicker basket. One Evie recognized from the Hillcrest House kitchen.

"What is all this?"

"I do believe you promised me a romantic dinner. Well, lunch in this case."

"I did but…I should have been the one to plan something." Not that she would have ever come up with something so romantic. "How did you manage all this?"

"I did have some help. We couldn't have our romantic meal without the chef being in on it, and Trisha volunteered to set this up. But the idea was all yours. I just picked the location."

As the saying went, location was everything. This out-of-the-way spot might have been an hour's drive from the hotel, but Evie felt a million miles away.

One day, she promised herself. One day to push all thoughts of the future and the past from her mind and to focus on the here and now. On this man. Right here. Right now.

Aaron had outdone himself. Mushroom issues aside, Evie didn't think the chef had ever made a richer, more decadent meal than the risotto paired with perfectly grilled asparagus and tender shrimp. And Trisha had thought of everything, packing the meal in insulated containers to keep everything warm and including plates, silverware and napkins along with a tiny bottle of champagne and two crystal flutes.

Griffin poured himself a few swallows and offered Evie the rest. Not that she needed the added alcohol. She already felt as if she might burst, bubbles of pure pleasure building up inside her as they talked and laughed throughout the meal. Awareness heightened with every shared look and touch and taste. Like when Griffin offered her a bite even though she had a dozen perfectly cooked shrimp on her own plate. Or when she reached over to brush a nonexistent crumb from the corner of his mouth and Griffin captured her thumb between his lips. Or when they took turns feeding each other chocolate mousse and strawberries.

As the fresh fruit and rich, creamy chocolate tempted her taste buds, and the surf crashed against the shore, Evie couldn't help letting out a slightly incredulous laugh. "This is by far the most romantic meal I've ever had."

As soon as she'd spoken the words, she ducked her head. This was anything but a typical Thursday for her, but for Griffin... Who knew? The man flew his own plane. He owned hotels around the world, in some of the most exotic and iconic locales. Though she'd wanted to leave the past behind, she couldn't help remembering Eric and how easily she'd fallen for him and how his over-the-top gestures had all been geared to blind her to his real motive. Not to win her heart but to steal her hotel.

"Hey." Running his finger along her jaw, Griffin turned her face toward him. "What's wrong?"

"Nothing. It's—" She gave a self-conscious laugh. "I

was thinking you probably do things like this all the time. My typical Thursday lunch is eating a turkey sandwich at my desk. But you already know that."

"I don't know that I have typical Thursdays. The last few months I've been in Dubai. Before that, it was Miami. Before that... I don't know if I even remember before that. But I know one thing. It wasn't here. It wasn't with you. And there is no place I'd rather be."

She wanted to believe him. She truly did. As he'd reminded her the night before, some things didn't need to be seen to be believed. Sometimes you just had to feel. And Evie felt this mattered to Griffin, that sharing his love of flying mattered. This wasn't some well-rehearsed seduction scene laid out numerous times with numerous women in Griffin's past.

And Evie wanted to know more about his love of flying. "When did you first realize you wanted to learn to fly?"

"The very first time I took the controls when I was fourteen."

"Come on. I'm serious."

"So am I," Griffin insisted, and she could see in his expression that he meant every word. "I was fourteen, and it was the day of my mother's funeral."

"Oh, I—I didn't realize."

He shrugged, but the tension in his broad shoulders told Evie he wasn't as unaffected as he tried to pretend. "It was a long time ago."

Though she wanted to ask what had happened, Evie decided to leave it to Griffin to tell her as much or as little as he chose. So instead she asked, "How did you end up behind the wheel—so to speak—when you were still a kid?"

The question chased the shadows from his expression,

and his smile was a reward in itself as he said, "That was thanks to my grandfather, my mother's dad. He was a pilot and had served in Vietnam. He was always tinkering on some old plane or another. He'd taken me up before, but that was the first day he let me take the controls, and from that moment, I was hooked."

Evie could imagine the scene—a boy and his grandfather, both mourning the woman they had lost, and a grandfather smart enough to realize how much his hurting grandson needed to take some small measure of control.

"He's the one, isn't he?" Evie asked suddenly.

"The one what?"

"The one who left you the inheritance."

That drew a small smile from him. "And how did you know about that?"

"Alexa may have mentioned something," Evie admitted.

"Yes. He left it to me in a trust. One that my father unfortunately controls."

"And what's the deal with that? Why is he still holding on to it? Are you that untrustworthy?"

Griffin laughed. "I'm sure if you ask him he'd agree with that. He thinks—hell, I don't know what he thinks. He's been holding it over my head for almost ten years. At first I figured he'd let it go when I was twenty-one, and then twenty-five."

"What would you have done if you father had given you that money at twenty or even twenty-five?" Evie asked with a knowing, teasing look.

"Invested wisely?"

"Yeah, I can imagine you 'investing' in every trendy hot-spot bar and club in LA."

Griffin had to admit that Evie was right. Unchecked, he likely would have blown through most of the money.

But that was then. "I'm almost thirty years old now, and he's still holding on to the trust like he's denying me my allowance. The James hotels are my legacy, but flying—that's my dream. If only my father could understand that."

If he'd expected some sort of understanding from Evie, he was setting himself up for disappointment. The look she shot him was dubious at best. "Come on, Griffin. You're a wealthy, successful man in your own right. You don't need your trust fund to go after your dream. You could start small on your own or find investors to back you. That you haven't..." She shrugged. "Well, it makes me wonder how serious you are about this."

Her words set off a spark of anger, reminding him how his father trivialized Griffin's flying as nothing more than a hobby. As if he were still a kid out playing with a remote control toy instead of a pilot behind the controls of his own craft. But unlike his father, Evie wasn't dismissing his dream. Instead she was challenging him to face the real reason he hadn't gone after it.

He thought of Kevin, his project assistant in Dubai, and how hard the kid had worked to show he was ready for the responsibility. He thought of Evie and how far she was willing to go to prove herself to her aunt and to keep Hillcrest House in the family.

All their efforts, all their determination, was focused on their own dreams.

Griffin worked hard, too, but all his efforts had centered around the James hotels. Was it any wonder his father saw his love of flying as nothing more than a hobby? Wasn't that how Griffin had been treating it, as something that took a distant second place to his "real" job?

"My grandfather started the business, but it was my

father who built it into the global company it is today. From the time I was a little kid, I knew that one day I would be expected to take over." He honestly thought he'd accepted his future, his fate, until a wake-up call had made him take a hard look at the man he'd become.

"Six months ago was the anniversary of my mother's death. And I missed it. Every year on that day, I try to do something to remember her. Usually I go up in a plane like I did the day of her funeral. But last year I was in Miami, trying to get a disaster of a hotel back on schedule. We were short staffed, over budget, struggling to replace incompetent subcontractors."

"It sounds like you had a lot on your mind," Evie said sympathetically.

"I did," Griffin admitted, "but too much of it was on the wrong things. When I first started working for the company, I thought I could take some of the burden of responsibility off my father. But when I realized I had missed the anniversary of my mother's death, I had to face facts. Instead of changing my dad, I was turning into him."

Griffin wasn't the type to spill his guts and certainly not to the women he dated. But the pressure eased from his chest as he admitted what he hadn't told another soul. "I don't know how to walk away from the family business without walking away from my father."

It was bad enough that he'd let down his mother. Would he have to let his father down, too?

He didn't realize he'd spoken the words aloud until Evie asked, "How could you possibly have let your mother down? You were only a boy."

"Before she died, I made my mom a promise. That I would make my father laugh, the way I had always made her laugh. But honestly? I can't even remember that last time I saw my father smile. And not only have I let my mother down, I've let myself down by not going after my own dreams."

Evie's heart ached at the raw emotion written on Griffin's face. She'd tried to convince herself that Griffin was a flirt, always joking around, never taking life seriously. She'd seen hints of another side to him, but she'd brushed those signs aside, unwilling to look beneath the surface.

Maybe he wasn't the shallow one. Maybe she was.

Griffin was a man who had lost his mother and lived his life trying to fulfill a boyhood promise. A promise to smile, to laugh, to make the people around him happy. A man who had put his father's dreams and goals and expectations in front of his own.

"It's not too late, you know."

She had seen him laugh and tease and joke, but behind the controls of the plane, he'd let all those superficial emotions fall go to embrace the freedom and pride and true joy he took in flying. Flying was something he loved, but was *something* enough?

"And as for the promise you made to your mother… what about you, Griffin?" she asked softly. "Who makes you laugh?"

He looked startled by the question, and the shields around her heart started to crack even more. No one had ever referred to her as the life of the party. She'd never been the type to tell jokes, never been the playful, flirtatious type. She was the one people went to when they wanted logical, practical advice. When they wanted someone to talk them out of foolish, reckless behavior.

But wasn't having fun part of her plan? Her aunt was right. Evie had been too focused on the hotel, too willing to let life pass her by until Griffin had come along.

Laughing, fun-loving Griffin was the one man, the only man, who could have made her crazy plan a success.

"Your mother would be very proud of you," she told him, but he was already shaking his head. And Evie knew some things had to be seen to be believed.

Grabbing his hand, she tugged him after her. "Come on!"

He followed at first, easily keeping up with her as she jogged and then ran across the beach. But as her mad dash neared the surf line where the sand was wet and cold, he slowed, holding her back as he asked, "Evie, what are you doing?"

She turned to face him as he pulled her to a stop. A slight smile tugged at his perfect lips, but that wasn't enough. Evie was all about goals, and this was one she was determined to reach. She leaned closer, watching the amused light in his eyes burn brighter as her breasts brushed against his chest and her breath feathered across those still-smiling lips. "I am...going for a swim!"

The shock on his face was priceless, and Evie took advantage of the moment to pull her hand from his and take off at a dead run toward the water.

Looking back over her shoulder, she laughed as Griffin half ran, half hopped after her as he tried pulling off his shoes and socks without breaking stride. "Are you crazy?"

Even with her head start and Griffin's footwear strip-tease, he caught up with her before her own toes had done more than hit the edge of the frigid surf. She sucked in a quick breath as cold water struck her skin like a thousand icy needles. Then she gasped again as Griffin scooped her up against his chest.

"Are you crazy?" he asked again, but this time he was laughing as he said it. The earlier shadows of the past had disappeared, and Evie didn't worry about Griffin having to hold her weight because she felt lighter than air at her accomplishment. She—straitlaced, oh-so-serious, stick-in-the-mud Evie McClaren—had made Griffin James laugh.

Giving a carefree shrug as she indulged in the pleasure of running her fingers through his hair, Evie said, "What? I felt like a swim."

"Oh, well, in that case…" Taking two giant steps into the waves, he swung his arms back in a rocking motion as if ready to toss her straight into the ocean.

Giving a girlish squeal, a sound Evie never thought she'd make in her adult life, she threw her arms around his shoulders. But Griffin merely spun them both around in a circle before letting go of her legs until she stood in front of him. The water was freezing, every icy splash stealing her breath, but Evie didn't care. The rush of the waves pushed her body into Griffin's before the receding undertow tried to pull her away. Through it all, his arms held her tight, anchoring her body to his against the ebb and flow.

The salty scent of the ocean mixed with Griffin's expensive, spicy aftershave, the combination drawing Evie closer to the warm skin of his neck. His pulse pounded along the strong column of his throat, and Evie couldn't resist the temptation of pressing her lips to that exact spot.

"Evie." His voice was a low growl of warning, but she took no notice, parting her lips to taste that small square inch of skin. This time she was the one who absorbed the shudder rocking his strong body in reaction to an attraction as elemental and irresistible as the tide. "Evie…"

He groaned her name again, and a shiver raced through her. One that had him pulling back to look down at her. "You're cold."

"No," she argued. Granted, she could no longer feel her feet, but that had more to do with her floating above the earth than it did with the salty water swirling around her calves.

"Yes," Griffin insisted. "But don't worry. I think I have a good idea how to warm you up."

Chapter Thirteen

"What is this place?" Evie asked as they stood on the porch of a small cabin.

The rustic structure was tucked away in a wooded area within walking distance of the airstrip. With its log exterior and green roof, the cabin blended in perfectly with the rugged surroundings.

Griffin switched the travel bag he'd grabbed from the plane to his left hand as he reached for the door handle. He always kept a duffel with a change of clothes in the plane in case he took off on a whim and decided to stay overnight wherever he landed. He hadn't anticipated using the change of clothes on this occasion.

He smiled. Of course, he hadn't anticipated Evie wanting to take a dip in the frigid ocean, either. They were both soaked from midthigh down. Granted, this was California and the temperature was in the low sixties, but swimming weather it was not. He still didn't know what had possessed Evie to rush into the surf. She couldn't have surprised him more.

"The owner of the airstrip told me I could use this place, in case the weather turned."

The front door was unlocked, as promised. Considering the cabin and airstrip were on a dozen or so acres of private property, that was no surprise. What did take Griffin completely off guard, however, was the sight that greeted him. As he hit the light switch, the room was bathed in the muted glow from a small but elegantly decorated Christmas tree in one corner. Silver and gold glass ornaments hung from nearly every branch. The colorful lights glinted off a pair of champagne flutes and a bottle on ice.

Despite her professed humbug attitude, Evie's smile beamed as brightly as the star on top of the tree as she stepped inside the small living area. "Just in case, huh?"

Griffin didn't know if he should take credit for the romantic arrangement or deny that he'd had any part in it. Settling on middle ground, he repeated, "Just in case."

Lowering his duffel bag onto the hardwood floor, he bent down and unzipped the top to pull out a pair of drawstring sweatpants. "Here. Put these on."

"Hmm," Evie held the oversize sweats against her slender legs. "Sexy."

"Take these, too." He held up a pair of long athletic socks. "There's nothing sexy about hypothermia."

Evie's husky laughter heated his blood and eliminated any possibility of him suffering from low body temperature as she accepted the clothes from him. "Unlike oversize sweatpants and athletic socks." The wry voice and slight smirk were typical Evie.

But the look in her eye as she tossed the clothes aside

made Griffin's heart thunder, pounding against the walls of his chest harder than the waves crashing against the shore. Something about Evie was different. She had an added confidence, a certainty in herself, in him, in knowing that what the two of them had together was real.

"Evie…"

Stepping closer, she said, "I can't believe you did all this for me. The champagne, the tree…"

Growing up as the son of a wealthy man, Griffin had coasted through life plenty of times—accepting what was given to him with little thought about what he'd done to earn it. But not now. Not this time with Evie. He wanted… He needed to know he deserved this woman. "I had help," he confessed. "A lot of help."

He'd wanted their meal to be a complete surprise, so he'd asked Trisha and Aaron to arrange the picnic on the beach and told them about the small cabin. He really had only intended to use the place if the weather was too cold. Clearly the other couple had had something else in mind when he mentioned the cabin was at his disposal… just in case.

"Trisha and Aaron…" he began.

"Trisha and Aaron didn't ask me to come with them today. They aren't the ones who shared their love of flying with me. They aren't the ones who found that gorgeous spot on the beach. You did that. All of that and more. You—" Evie swallowed and a tender smile trembled on her lips as she whispered, "You make me laugh, Griffin. You make me happy."

And just like that, the emotions building inside him became a tsunami. Rushing beyond all walls, all barriers. Too strong, too powerful, too overwhelming for any possible defense to hold them back. "Evie—"

The words rushed up inside him, the promise to spend the rest of his life making her happy. Maybe being rich had made him greedy. He wanted all of her tomorrows. But Evie hadn't offered him a lifetime.

She'd only given him a day.

A better man, a stronger man, might have held out for more, but Griffin would take what he could get. He would grab hold of today and do everything in his power to make sure Evie still wanted him when the sun rose in the morning.

Reaching up, she cupped the back of his neck, her slender fingers cool against skin that felt on fire. "When you told me you had a way to warm me up, sweatpants were not what I had in mind."

The look in her sapphire-blue eyes was enough to set off a slow burn inside Griffin. Her hair was tousled from the ocean breeze and from her run on the beach. The dark strands were too short and too straight to truly run wild. Compared to the woman he'd met three months ago—a woman whose razor-sharp hairstyle matched her razor-sharp wit—this Evie was reckless and daring and even more irresistible. Her silk shirt was untucked. Salt water dampened the hem of her straight black skirt. Sand coated her slender feet and he had no idea where she'd left her shoes.

He ran his fingers through that wind-tossed hair, tucking the silken strands behind her ears. "I could…build a fire in the fireplace."

"Very romantic," Evie murmured, "but still not what I was thinking."

"Run you a hot bath?"

"Hmm…getting warmer."

"Take off all of these damp clothes?"

"Now, that's what I call hot."

* * *

Evie's heart pounded as Griffin captured her in a kiss as heated as any she could have hoped for, dreamed of, imagined. It was as though every other kiss had built toward the perfection of this one. She could still taste the sweetness from their earlier dessert mixed with the salt from their near dip in the ocean and a spice that was 100 percent Griffin's own.

She fisted her hands in his shirt, her body aching to get closer to his. "Griffin." She all but groaned his name and felt a shudder work through him in response. The tremble in those strong muscles gave Evie a feeling of power that was as heady and potent as his kiss, emboldening her to find the hem of his shirt and lay claim to the smooth warm skin of his back.

"Too many clothes, remember?"

Reaching back with one hand, he grabbed hold of the material and stripped away the shirt in one smooth, decidedly masculine motion. The flicker of candlelight played against his tanned skin, and for a moment Evie could only stare at the broad shoulders, perfectly honed abs and dusting of hair across his chest.

Swallowing, Evie admitted, "You were right, you know."

"Was I? About what?"

"The first night we met…I really did want to take your shirt off."

"Well, sweetheart, why didn't you say something? We could have ended up here a whole lot sooner."

But despite the words, despite his quick removal of his own clothes, Griffin seemed determined to take his time when it came to hers. She couldn't wait to feel his hands against her skin, and yet she didn't know if Griffin could move any slower. His fingers slid down the

V neckline of her shirt to the buttons that trembled between her breasts.

Goose bumps danced across her chest, but Evie was anything but cold. By the time he pushed the silk from her shoulders, she was almost surprised steam wasn't rising from her skin. She didn't give him the option of turning her skirt into some kind of lingering striptease. She made quick work of the zipper and let the garment fall to her feet, leaving her clad in nothing more than a black lace bra and matching panties.

"I was right about that first night, too, you know."

Desire had roughened his voice, and Evie could practically feel the scrape against her exposed nerve endings. "About what?"

"The first night we met, I was sure that beneath that sleek skirt and the oh-so-professional blouse buttoned to your throat you were wearing some of the sexiest satin and lace I'd ever hope to see."

"Good thing I'm not wearing boring old cotton," she teased.

It wasn't like her to exchange sexy banter while standing nearly naked in front of a man. But neither was it like her to skip out on work to fly off to a secluded beach or go running fully clothed into the ocean. This was her one day, and she was certainly making the most of it.

"Wouldn't matter," Griffin vowed as his big hands spanned the small of her back and he pulled her body tight to his. "All that would have done was prove how foolish I was not to realize how sexy cotton could be."

Maybe it was just a line. Maybe it was the type of thing Griffin James would say to any woman standing half-naked in front of him, but the raw honesty in his expression urged Evie to believe every word.

She clung to his broad shoulders as the trembling

muscles in her legs threatened to give way, but then it didn't matter if she was falling because Griffin was there to lower her to the soft pillows scattered across the floor. He trailed heated kisses down her throat to the swell of her breasts before brushing the garment aside.

Each gasping breath she took brought her closer to his openmouthed caresses. Her back arched, drawn to the pleasure of his touch, as his lips trailed lower across the sensitive skin of her stomach. Her muscles trembled and tightened as he stripped off the last barrier of satin and lace. He broke away only long enough to toss his own pants aside and grab protection. The lights from the tree illuminated him, and Evie's breath caught at the sight of such masculine perfection.

His lean body covered her, claimed her as he touched every part, and a wild rush of emotion threatened to overwhelm her. Evie had to look away, to close her eyes against the raw honesty she couldn't bring herself to trust.

But as Griffin had pointed out before, some things didn't need to be seen to be believed. Closing her eyes only made the passion in Griffin's kiss, the intensity of his body stroking deep within hers, that much harder to resist.

"Evie." His deep voice murmuring her name was as intimate and seductive as everything that had come before it. "Open your eyes."

She was helpless to deny his command, as helpless as she was to deny the building pleasure inside her. Any hope of holding on to some thread of control, of holding back some tiny part of herself, was lost as she shattered around him, the pleasure breaking in a brilliant burst that brought Griffin with her.

A faint buzz pulled Evie from a heavy slumber. Had she switched her phone alarm to Vibrate? She reached out blindly for her nightstand, wanting to slap the annoying sound into submission, but it wasn't wicker furniture her hand came in contact with as she threw an arm out across the bed.

Warm skin… Smooth muscles… *Griffin.*

Evie jerked into a sitting position. Blinking the sleep from her eyes, she felt her cheeks start to flame as she met his amused grin. Despite the tousled disarray of his dark blond hair and the early-morning stubble shadowing his jaw, he was clearly wide-awake and had been for some time… Doing what? Watching her sleep?

After making love in the living room, they had eventually managed to find their way to the bed. The shyness she hadn't felt the night before washed over her as he glanced down, and she clutched the sheet to her breasts. In her haste, she tugged a little too hard, stealing his side of the covers and leaving even more of all that warm skin and smooth muscle exposed.

"Morning, sweetheart."

The buzzing continued over the pulse pounding in her ears, and Evie swallowed. "Is that—I need to find my phone." She tried to scramble from the bed but stopped short, tethered to the spot by the corner of the sheet still tucked beneath Griffin's hip.

Chuckling, he reached out one tanned arm and tugged, giving Evie little choice but to tumble back beside him. "Relax," he said as he brushed her lips with a kiss. "That isn't your phone. It's mine."

"Oh. Well, aren't you going to answer it?" she asked, but the buzzing had stopped. At least, the one coming from his phone had. A different sort of vibration hummed along Evie's nerve endings as his kiss trailed across her jaw and down the length of her throat. Her hold on the sheet loosened as he murmured, "I can think of better things to do…like keeping you here forever."

Her hand tightened on the sheet. Forever wasn't part of the plan. Just one day and one night. One night of— yes, she would admit it now—pure magic that she would never forget. One night that would be enough to last her in the days and nights and *years* that stretched out in front of her.

Griffin James was gorgeous, sexy, exciting and unpredictable, and she should be glad that, for even a brief moment in time, he'd been hers.

But he didn't fit into her logical, well-ordered world any more than she could fit into his jet-setting, whirlwind life. What had he told her about Hillcrest House that first morning? The old-fashioned, solid, staid hotel didn't fit the James brand? Well, neither did she.

"Evie?" he asked. "What's going on in that big beautiful brain of yours?"

"We really need to get back to the hotel."

"Hillcrest House will survive without you."

But she wouldn't survive without the hotel. Her aunt was right that her job had become her refuge, her escape from living and loving, and once Griffin moved on, she would need it more than ever. "The whole point of this was so that it doesn't have to."

"The whole point of this…" he echoed slowly as he pulled away to lean back against the wooden headboard.

Evie gave a short laugh, the only pretending she'd done since Griffin had taken her hand the day before. She gestured toward the tangled sheets between them. "Well, not of *this*, but you know what I mean."

She expected a joke or at the very least a flippant comment in response. But Griffin held her eyes until her heart started to pound. She had to look away before he finally muttered, "Yeah, I'm starting to think I do."

"Griffin…" She didn't like knowing she'd hurt him. Didn't like knowing that she could. She'd spent so much time reminding herself that their relationship was strictly pretend, that she didn't dare fall in love, she'd never considered that Griffin might forget, that he might be the one to fall. She opened her mouth, completely unsure of what she might say, but the phone buzzed again before she had a chance. This time he swung his legs over the side of the bed and reached for his cell on the nightstand.

With his back turned to her as he barked out a greeting, Evie used the moment to slip away and escape into the bathroom. Maybe it was cowardly of her, but she needed some space, some distance to regain her perspective on everything that had happened the night before. Not an easy thing to do when confronted with the sight of her bra and panties draped over the shower rod.

She had no idea when Griffin had slipped out of bed to hang their wet things up to dry, but there they were. In all their satin-and-lace glory, the sexiest Griffin had ever hoped to see.

Evie grabbed her underwear along with her slacks and blouse, both wrinkled beyond recognition, and quickly pulled them on. She tried not to spare more than a glance at her reflection in the mirror above the sink. She hardly looked all buttoned-up and professional now.

"Evie."

She jumped at the sudden knock and barely had a second to prepare before Griffin swung the door open. His normally teasing grin was nowhere in sight as his gaze tracked from her rumpled hair down to her bare feet. The slacks he'd pulled on were in bad shape, too, but he hadn't bothered with a shirt. She tried to keep from ogling all that glorious tanned skin, but nothing could stop the dizzying memories of clutching those broad shoulders as his body moved in time with hers...

"The call wasn't for me," he said as he held out his cell, his expression one Evie couldn't quite read. "It's for you. Your cousin."

She fumbled with the phone as if unfamiliar with holding one rather than treating it like the extension of her hand it had practically become. "Hello?"

She stepped back into the bedroom, aware of the sound of the door latch catching behind her. Turning, she realized she was alone. Griffin had given her the privacy she'd been looking for earlier, and she should have been grateful. But she couldn't help feeling a door of a different kind had closed between them.

"Evie? Where on earth have you been?" Rory demanded.

"I'm..." Evie's voice stalled with the realization that she didn't know exactly where they were. How had a plan that seemed so simple and straightforward gotten so far off course that she literally had no idea where she was?

Fortunately, Rory didn't wait for an answer Evie couldn't give. "I've been texting you for the past two hours."

Texting her? Evie reached a hand into her pocket, but her phone wasn't there. Even worse, she didn't know where it was. Had it fallen out when she ran along the beach? When Griffin had teasingly threatened to toss her into the waves? When he'd stripped off her clothes and made love to her among the pillows still scattered like presents in front of the Christmas tree? "I—I...misplaced my phone."

Silence echoed across the line for so long Evie thought—hoped?—they'd been disconnected. But then her cousin's incredulous voice echoed, "Misplaced it?"

For the past two years, that phone and everything it represented—her commitment to her job, her 24/7 connection to her career—had meant everything to her. And for her to let it slip from her hand without a single thought...

"It was only one day," she whispered. One day to let go. To have fun. To laugh...to love...

But what was supposed to have been a harmless escape now seemed reckless, irresponsible, dangerous. One day. All it had taken was one day for her to forget...everything.

"Look, Evie..." Her cousin's voice was different now, calm and cool, the voice she used when she talked down hysterical would-be brides on the verge of emotional explosions. "It's going to be okay."

The soothing tone had a different effect on Evie. Because despite her pseudo almost engagement, she wasn't a Hillcrest House bride. She wasn't hysterical. And *dammit*, she was not emotional!

Gritting her back teeth, she demanded, "What's wrong?"

"I shouldn't have called."

"But you did," Evie pointed out, glad to hear that her voice was calm, too, and if not cool, then...*cold*. "And you wouldn't have unless something was wrong. So what is it? A problem with one of the guests? A problem with the wedding?"

"Not the guests." Rory sighed, and Evie sensed her cousin's regret. She also sensed that Rory knew Evie wouldn't let her off the hook without telling everything. "It's Aaron and Trisha."

Evie blinked. She hadn't expected that. After seeing them together the night of the festival, after the wonderful meal they'd helped Griffin arrange and all the romantic touches decorating the cabin, she'd thought...

What? That the hotel's magic was real and they would live happily-ever-after?

"I should have known something like this would happen," she muttered.

"From what Aunt E's been telling me, you did. You spotted it when the rest of us thought they couldn't stand each other."

The couple's constant bickering, their supposed disdain for each other, was all an act. Evie had seen through it all because she'd gotten rather good at playing a role herself.

Pretending to be falling for Griffin...

Or was it pretending she *wasn't* falling for Griffin?

Rubbing the ache building behind her forehead, she asked, "How bad was the fallout from the breakup?"

"Breakup? Evie, Trisha and Aaron didn't break up." Evie heard the deep breath her cousin took, and her hand tightened on the phone. Whatever had happened was somehow worse, much worse, than she'd imagined. "They eloped."

Chapter Fourteen

"I'm so sorry!" The wobble of tears filled Trisha's voice, coming from the speakerphone in Evie's office. Evie, Rory and their aunt, along with Chance and Alexa, had all gathered there for a conference call once Rory had finally gotten hold of Trisha. Not at the Reno Chapel of Love, but at the regional hospital.

"We left yesterday morning and were supposed to be back home in plenty of time for the rehearsal dinner tonight. We had it all planned," the distraught woman cried.

Evie sucked in a deep breath. Ah, yes, she knew all about plans. And all about the *but-thens* that could throw such sudden curves that you were left spinning out of control.

Like the way she'd lost such total control in Griffin's arms.

Her cheeks burned, and she felt sure her entire family could see what she and Griffin had been doing in the hours while she was away from Hillcrest House. If not on her face, then certainly in her wrinkled, morning-after clothes. She should have stopped at the cottage first, but with her focus on damage control, she'd asked Griffin to take her directly to the hotel. Which he'd done. With barely a word spoken between them.

There'd been no scenic route taken during the flight back. No cruising the ruggedly beautiful coastline, no trying to spot wildlife on the edge of the towering redwoods, no searching for whales in the Pacific.

Griffin had her feet back on solid ground in no time, and that was where she belonged. As much as she wanted to be the carefree woman on the beach, the one willing to toss aside her shoes along with her common sense, that wasn't really who she was. At least, not at Hillcrest House.

Here people counted on her for her cool head, for her logic, for her ability to handle a crisis. Here people counted on her for their livelihoods and to keep the history of the Victorian hotel alive and well. Here she had more important things to do than to try to make a man laugh.

Evie knew it. Judging by Griffin's silence as she'd walked away, he did, too. So why did the very thought make her want to cry?

"…food poisoning," Trisha was saying. "Aaron didn't want to go to the hospital, but I was afraid he was getting dehydrated. The emergency room is packed. We've been waiting for hours, and they've just taken Aaron back to see the doctor. They're going to give him some IV fluids, but I'm not sure how long they'll want to keep him. By the time we make the drive back—"

"Trisha, stop," Aunt E cut in. "You've both been up

for twenty-four hours. Neither of you is going to be in any shape for a long drive."

"But the wedding…" Trisha's voice broke on the word, and Chance and Alexa exchanged a glance before reaching over to take each other's hands.

"We'll figure it out," her aunt insisted. "You take care of that husband of yours. We've got everything here under control."

Under control? Evie dug her fingernails into her palms as she clenched her fists. She'd never felt so completely *out* of control.

Once Trisha said her goodbyes and disconnected the call, a stunned silence followed. "I still can't believe they eloped," Rory stated. "I mean, I really thought they couldn't stand each other."

"Love is a funny thing," their aunt mused. "Isn't it, Evie?"

Funny? Her own voice whispered through her ears along with the distant sound of waves crashing against the shoreline. *You make me laugh, Griffin. You make me happy.*

Evie swallowed. That didn't make it love.

"You don't seem all that surprised by this," Chance added. "Did you know something the rest of us didn't?"

Guilt weighed on Evie's chest, making it hard to breathe. She had known. And instead of putting a stop to it, she'd actually encouraged the relationship.

"Oh, Chance." Alexa blinked back tears, and Evie braced herself. The woman was engaged *and* pregnant and as deserving of a breakdown as a bride could be. "This is all just so…*romantic*!"

Evie's jaw dropped as Chance responded with a goofy grin and leaned over to kiss his fiancée. "Almost as romantic as the night we met and I held you in my arms on the dance floor for the very first time. Don't you think?"

Evie thought they'd both lost their minds. "Romantic?" she echoed. "Have you forgotten that you're getting married tomorrow and that Aaron is the hotel's chef? Without him—"

"We're still getting married," Chance interrupted, his gaze still locked with Alexa's. "You can serve hot dogs for all I care."

"Hot dogs. Right. That's the answer. We'll serve the hotel's most important and influential guests processed mystery meat on a bun." The pulse pounded so loudly in her ears, Evie was almost surprised the hotel's stained-glass windows weren't shaking from the reverberations.

There was only one thing she could do. The same thing she had done when she discovered Eric's true motives. She had to stand up and take responsibility for her actions...for her mistakes. Looking each of them in the eye, Evie said, "I'm sorry. This is all my fault. I should have been more on top of things. If I had been—"

"If you had been, then what?" Chance challenged. "Come on, Evie, I know you like to think you're in charge of *everything* around here, but do you really think you have the power to stop people from falling in love?"

Pacing the length of the patterned carpet outside Evie's office, Griffin tried to stay calm. After such a glorious night, he'd woken up to one hell of a morning. The distant look in Evie's expression, the phone call, the tense flight back. God, he'd hated letting her walk away to face her family on her own.

Letting her...

The scoffing laugh got caught somewhere in his chest,

right around the ragged edges of his heart. She'd all but dismissed him without a backward glance.

During the ride from the airstrip, Evie had used the small mirror in the passenger visor to fix her hair and apply a touch of makeup, piling on as much professionalism as she could pack from the slim black purse she carried. By the time he pulled up to the front of the hotel, he was half-surprised she hadn't thanked him with a tip.

The sound of the door opening ricocheted through his body like a bullet, and Griffin turned to watch Alexa and the rest of the McClarens file out of Evie's office. Instead of following her family toward the lobby, Evie glanced his way. Only Griffin didn't get the sense she was looking at him, but more that she was looking past him. The emptiness on her face sent a feeling of panic plunging through him as he walked toward her. "Evie."

Shaking her head, she held out a hand as if to keep him at a distance. So different from the way she'd pulled him closer in the isolated cabin the day before. "I can't talk right now, Griffin."

As much as it hurt, her withdrawal wasn't a total surprise. Reaching into his pocket, he pulled out what he hoped might be an icebreaker. "I found your phone tucked between the car seats."

"I—thank you." She swiped her thumb across the screen and winced, no doubt at all the texts from her cousin that she'd missed.

"What did you find out about Trisha and Aaron?"

After giving the brief explanation, she added, "Evidently our romance inspired them." Her lips twisted into a mocking smile that sent a strike straight to his heart. "They headed for Nevada after setting up the picnic on the beach."

Griffin ran a frustrated hand through his hair. "You

don't really believe we had anything to do with that. How many wedding dinners has Aaron cooked? How many ceremonies has Trisha helped plan? If none of that 'inspired' them, I don't see how we could have." Not that he would have cared if seeing Evie and him together had somehow made the other couple realize they'd fallen in love.

Hell, he wished it worked both ways and Evie might figure out she loved him. As much as he... Griffin cut off the thought before it formed. He already felt as though he were flying blind through uncharted territory. He didn't dare take his hands off the controls now.

"If I'd been here—" Cutting herself off, she bit down on her lower lip. Her lipstick was a bright fuchsia, reminding him of the flowers he'd sent her, of the bougainvillea with its delicate blooms and dangerous thorns that could so easily draw blood.

"If you'd been here instead of with me. That's what you're saying, right? That this is my fault."

"No, of course not! It's just—you don't understand how important this is to me!"

After all they'd shared, that accusation hurt more than Griffin thought possible. How many times had his father laid that same complaint at his feet? Griffin didn't take his career, his legacy, his responsibility to the James hotels seriously enough.

Griffin knew what was important. His mother had taught him that, and it wasn't a glass-and-steel high-rise in Dubai and it wasn't a gorgeous Victorian in small-town Clearville. "Is that really what you think?"

"I think—I maybe think my aunt was right," she whispered. "Maybe I can't have Hillcrest and a life."

Turning down the hall, she all but ran from him. Swearing beneath his breath, Griffin rushed after her.

He caught up with her on the front porch, as easily as he had the day before, but this time Evie wasn't laughing. Her chest rose and fell as she sucked in the cool morning air, and Griffin wasn't surprised she was out of breath.

She'd been running since early that morning.

It wasn't as obvious now as it had been when she'd practically jumped naked from the bed, but he still sensed her withdrawal in her rigid, professional stance. That he wanted to hold on when he was always the first in a relationship to let go told Griffin how far gone he really was.

Has there ever been something you wanted so badly you can picture it perfectly, and yet it's always out of reach?

When Evie asked that question that first night at the bar, he'd thought he'd known then. He damn well did now. After all these years, Griffin finally understood why his mother had tasked him with the goal of making the people around him laugh. She'd wanted him to be able to hold on to the carefree joy of his childhood and not to be burdened by the sorrow of her passing. But somewhere along the way, Griffin had stopped being carefree and become careless. He'd refused to allow anyone close enough to take hold of his heart.

Until he met Evie.

There was nothing he wouldn't do for her. And while he might not know what it was like to *want* to run his family's hotels, he had plenty of experience doing so.

"I know you only gave me one day, but is there any chance you brought a little bit of that trust in me back from the beach with you?"

Her dark eyebrows drew together in a frown. "Did I—what?"

Stepping closer, he ran a finger along her jawline, tilting her face up. "Do you trust me, Evie?"

His voice was low, as though weighed down by the magnitude behind the words and by his very future hanging in the balance.

Her eyes were wide, the midnight depths filled with emotion as she swallowed. He knew it wasn't an easy ask, not after what her ex had put her through. But he needed to know he'd earned her trust even as his conscience reminded him that he didn't completely deserve it.

"There might be a few grains still stuck in my shoes."

Griffin didn't know when such a slightly teasing comment had made him want to throw back his head and laugh more. He longed to pick Evie up and sweep her into his arms like he had when she'd shocked the hell out of him by running into the surf. He contented himself by pouring all the emotions inside him—all the words he couldn't say—into one perfect kiss. "You won't regret it," he pledged against her lips. "I promise."

"What are you going to do?"

Griffin gave a wry smile as he straightened. "I know this is your line, but I have a plan."

Later that morning, after taking a desperately needed shower and changing into a no-frills, all-business outfit that made her at least *look* put together, Evie met with the kitchen staff. Most were as stunned as her family had been about Aaron and Trisha's sudden elopement and all of them looked to Evie for answers she didn't have.

"How bad is it?" Rory asked as she sank into the chair across from Evie's desk.

"We should be fine for the rehearsal dinner tonight. Aaron brought in the makings for a stone fruit and goat cheese salad, with salmon and broccolini for the entrée. But the wedding…" The queasy feeling in the pit of her stomach made her wish for a case of food poisoning of her own. "No one seems to know exactly what he had planned for the reception. Chance and Alexa, in the throes of their romantic bliss, evidently decided that Aaron could surprise them. So...surprise!"

"I'm sure the staff will come up with something," her cousin said.

"Something," Evie muttered. But not the kind of meal that would impress the wealthy guests who would be attending Alexa and Chance's wedding. Not the kind that would impress Alexa's hard-to-please and influential grandmother.

Trust me.

Evie had trusted Griffin. With her life as he took the controls of his plane. With her body as they made love. But with her heart? With Hillcrest House?

That idea scared her far more than soaring through the clouds at several thousand feet or stripping naked in an out-of-the-way cabin. The last time she'd given a man that kind of trust, she'd lost everything. Not just her heart. Not just the opportunity to run the hotel. Not just the money to pay for a wedding that never happened.

She'd lost her faith, her hope, her trust. In love, in happily-ever-after, in herself. She had always been the smart one, from the time she was a little girl. So how could she possibly have been so stupid as to fall for Eric? Maybe she wasn't so smart after all. Maybe she didn't deserve this second shot to follow her dream.

Trust me.

And wasn't there, despite everything, a part of her that wanted to do just that? To trust in whatever Griffin had in mind even as she met with the kitchen staff to come up with a backup plan of her own?

"Maybe if we call Aaron, he could—" Evie cut herself off as she caught sight of the disbelieving and disapproving lift to Rory's dark eyebrows. "What?" she demanded. "It's not like he's actually on his honeymoon."

"No, he's actually in the hospital with food poisoning." Standing up, Rory circled around the desk to lean one hip against its smooth surface. "Is everything okay between you and Griffin?"

"Why do you ask?"

"The last few days, you've been acting so un-Evie. And seeing you and Griffin together, the way he looks at you... I had my doubts at first, but I want you to know I couldn't be happier for you."

Evie swallowed back the tears gathering in the back of her throat as her cousin bent to give her a wildflower-scented hug. She didn't know why she was getting emotional when Rory was always so free with her affections, hugging perfect strangers given the chance. But her cousin's happiness for her only magnified Evie's mixed-up feelings.

Stiffening in her cousin's embrace, she said, "As wonderful as Hillcrest House is, there's no magic here that makes people fall in love."

Rory gave a little laugh as she leaned back. "How can you say that after everything that's happened? First me and Jamison, and then Chance and Alexa. Now with Trisha and Aaron eloping? Not to mention the most powerful proof of all."

She grinned, looking exactly as she had when they were children and she knew something Evie didn't. "Who would ever have thought my cynical, anti-love cousin would fall in love and get engaged after such a whirlwind romance? You can't tell me that isn't Hillcrest magic!"

"It's a lie."

Rory's smile faded into confusion. "What are you talking about?"

Shoving back from her desk, Evie stood and ran both of her hands through her hair as she paced the small office. "Everything about my relationship with Griffin has been a lie. Convincing everyone that Griffin and I are a couple when—when we're not."

Evie hadn't planned to say the words, hadn't planned to admit the truth to anyone until the charade was over—and maybe not even then. But it was better this way. Better that Rory knew the truth and stopped believing that what Evie and Griffin had was love. Stopped the ridiculous hints about engagements and weddings. Stopped thinking that Griffin's teasing words, heated looks and soul-stealing touches were anything more than temporary. She needed to stop believing in happily-ever-after when Evie knew it wasn't true.

Rory frowned. "Why would you do that? Any of that?"

"It's all Aunt E's fault." Filling Rory in on the business meeting that had taken place over a month ago, Evie concluded with, "So, you see? From the moment Griffin stepped out of my bathroom wearing nothing but a towel, the whole thing has been all for show."

"All of it except for one thing, Evie." Reaching out, Rory caught Evie's arm as she stalked by and gave an understanding squeeze. "You did a pretty good job fooling the family, but something tells me you've done an even better job fooling yourself."

"What do you mean?"

"I know you, and, sweetie, you're not that good of an actress. Somewhere along the way you stopped pretending to be in love and started falling in love instead."

Chapter Fifteen

The sun was sinking into the ocean, painting the sky a gorgeous sorbet-colored mix of orange and pink and purple as the wedding party gathered inside the gleaming white tent for the rehearsal dinner. Though the forecast promised rain, the weather had held so far and Evie hoped at least that much continued to go their way.

A white lattice arbor stood on a dais, the spot where Chance and Alexa would exchange vows before moving into the hotel ballroom for their reception. The flowers would arrive in the morning—garlands to drape the archway, small sprays to decorate the back of each chair, along with centerpieces for each table for the reception.

Everything was perfect, poised and waiting, for this final walk-through…except for one thing.

"Griffin didn't say where he was going? Or when he'd be back?" Worry pulled at Alexa's eyebrows as she stared hopefully at Evie and clutched Chance's hand.

"I'm sure he'll be here," she promised. "He has a plan."

Her cousin frowned in response. "A plan? What kind of plan?"

Evie had no idea, and yet she was somehow counting on it. On Griffin. "Look, Chance—"

"Hey, everyone, let the wedding march begin!"

The three of them turned at the sound of the familiar voice filling the tent. Griffin stepped inside, looking gorgeous and slightly windswept, grinning as if he knew they'd been waiting for him.

The way she'd been waiting her whole life for someone like him...

Chance had no such patience. "Where the hell have you been?"

"Picking up a last-minute wedding present," Griffin said as he held his hand out and spoke quietly to someone standing behind him.

Evie wasn't sure what she had expected, but it wasn't the petite blonde who stepped inside the tent with a tentative smile and uncertain wave. "Um, hi, everyone."

"This is Simone d'Arnaud. She is—was," Griffin corrected himself with a slightly chagrined smile, "the executive chef at the James hotel in Carmel before she decided to open her own catering company. She has graciously agreed to fill in for Aaron while he's on his honeymoon."

"I thought he was in the hospital," Simone whispered in an aside that carried throughout the tent.

Griffin shrugged. "In this case, same thing." Catching Evie's attention, he offered an audacious wink that set her pulse pounding.

A chef. He'd found another chef. And not just any chef, since Evie was certain James Hotels would hire the best of the best. He'd come through for her in a way that only

Griffin James possibly could. The trust she'd placed in him had been rewarded—with a Michelin star.

All around her, the bridal party was thanking Griffin for saving day—even Chance grudgingly offered his hand. Griffin, being Griffin, shrugged off the gratitude, but she could see the pleasure he took in making the people around him smile.

It took everything in her not to rush straight to him, throw her arms around his neck and kiss him just like she had on the beach. Just like a woman in love…

Only she wouldn't. Because she wasn't.

Somewhere along the way you stopped pretending…

Rory would think that. It was practically her job to think that, but Evie knew better.

Yes, Griffin had flown in to save the day, but soon he would fly away. To Miami or Dubai or Japan. Or maybe he would even pursue his own dream and a career separate from his father's—a career that would still have him flying off to exotic, exciting locales.

Either way, he was bound to leave, but until then… Until then, who would blame her if she closed her eyes and let herself pretend that Christmas wishes really came true?

"I don't know how to thank you for this," she told him as he made his way over to her while the rest of the bridal party took their places.

"Maybe you should wait until you've actually had a chance to try Simone's food."

"I don't need to wait, Griffin." Brushing a kiss filled with promise against his lips, she whispered, "I already know how amazing it's going to be."

As the bridal party raved over a mouthwatering meal of perfectly blackened salmon, creamy garlic parmesan potatoes and tender-crisp broccolini, Griffin slipped out the French doors and onto the balcony.

He dialed his father's number only to disconnect the call and shove the phone back into his pocket at the sound of the recorded voice. Had his father been someone else, Griffin might have thought his father had turned his phone off. But his father was Frederick James, and every day was a workday. His phone was never out of reach, so Griffin knew his father had received each of his messages and was choosing not to return a single one.

Blowing out a frustrated breath, he gripped the cold metal railing along the balcony and breathed in air tinged with the slightest hint of woodsmoke from a distant fireplace. He turned at the click of the latch behind him to see Evie step outside. Earlier in the evening, she'd shed her suit jacket, leaving her clad in a straight skirt and an elegant ivory blouse that bared her slender arms. Her skin gleamed like alabaster, her eyes as dark as the night sky.

"What are you doing out here?" She tilted her head, gesturing to the room behind her. "You're about to miss out on dessert. And after that dinner, skipping dessert would be something of a crime. Are all the James hotel chefs so amazing?"

"Simone is an incredible chef. We tried to convince her to stay, but she left to follow her dream."

And it was time he did the same. Even if his father never understood, even if Frederick never forgave him, Griffin had to chart his own course. Maybe Evie was right; maybe his father had held on to the ties to his trust as a way to hold on to him, but he couldn't stay grounded, tethered to the legacy of James Hotels any longer.

But before he said anything about his own plans, he wanted to make sure his father kept his distance from Hillcrest House. Evie seemed confident that she'd done enough to convince her aunt that both the hotel and her love life were in good hands. Griffin hoped she was right. Because he was done. Done *pretending* he was falling in love.

His heart stalled as she moved closer, then revved like a turbojet engine as she placed her hands on his chest. "I still can't believe you did this."

"You would have come up with something."

She gave a small laugh, her hair falling forward to curtain her face. "Chance's bright idea was to serve hot dogs," she murmured.

"See?" Brushing the silken strands back, he added, "You already had a backup plan in place."

A hint of vulnerability softened her expression as she admitted, "He said he didn't care what we served. All that mattered was that he and Alexa were getting married."

"Well, I never thought I'd say this, but Chance is right. Love is all that matters."

"Careful," Evie warned. "Don't let Rory hear you say that or she'll think you've been touched by Hillcrest's magic."

"It wasn't the hotel's magic, Evie." He stared into her midnight eyes, feeling like some long-ago explorer relying on the constellations in the sky for his bearings. He searched for some sign, some glimmer that Evie felt the same way he did. Without that star to guide him, he would be well and truly lost.

But she only laughed, not taking his words seriously, not taking *him* seriously, and it killed him a little that even now she wouldn't admit what Griffin knew was true in his heart. "Of course not. There's no such thing."

The words he'd spoken during their dance at the Holly and Vine event echoed in his mind. *Those who don't believe in magic will never bother to look...* Frustrated,

Griffin didn't know how to make Evie see what was right in front of her.

Or maybe she did see it, because hadn't he heard something off in her laughter? Something the slightest bit brittle around the edges that told him she was trying a little too hard? That she was pretending.

"Evie…"

She stopped him, afraid, perhaps, of what he might say by wrapping her slender arms around his neck. "If you're not interested in dessert in the dining room, maybe we can take something to go."

Griffin didn't have any trouble reading what Evie was offering as she rose to her toes to brush her lips against his in a kiss that tasted like champagne. The instant flare of desire marked a path that would be so easy to pursue. A familiar road he'd traveled so many times before with other women. Sinking his fingers into the warm fall of her hair, Griffin kissed her. Pouring everything he felt, everything he hadn't said, into the kiss, into the sweet, slow seduction of his lips against hers.

No such thing as magic? Evie might as well have dismissed the very air he breathed…

Her body swayed, drawn closer by the emotion she denied, even as Griffin broke the kiss. His body thrummed with desire, ready to follow wherever Evie led, just as he'd promised, but the rules of the game had changed.

"I told you once that when I kissed you for the first time, it wouldn't be pretend." Sucking in a deep breath of the cool evening air, he managed a wry smile. "Well, when I take you to bed for the second time, I want that to be real, too."

When I take you to bed for the second time…
"Ugh! It's not like I asked him to take me to bed," Evie

muttered to herself as she stalked across the crushed-gravel path from the cottage to the hotel, the plastic garment bag slung over one arm crinkling with each step.

At least not in so many words.

In a few minutes, she would have to put on her beautiful bridesmaid's dress along with her happy bridesmaid's smile, but she had yet to work out her…frustration over the way things had ended with Griffin the night before.

I want that to be real, too.

"And it's not like I faked anything!" she continued, her argument gaining a head of steam.

Every kiss, every sigh, every caress had been real and raw and honest.

But that wasn't what Griffin meant, and she knew it.

He wasn't talking about making love; he was talking about *being* in love. But what would it matter and why would he care unless…

Was it possible that Griffin had feelings for her? Real, raw, honest feelings for her?

"There you are!" Rory called out the moment Evie stepped into the bridal room at the back of the hotel and stopped short.

Everything inside her screamed to run away as she took in the five women in various states of undress, talking and laughing as they crowded around the vanity table and mirrors with every possible form of curler, hair dryer and straightening iron known to humankind in use.

"Do not make me go in there," she muttered to her cousin as Rory took her arm and started pulling her into the madness. With everyone crammed into the small space, Evie didn't know how she was supposed to find room to breathe let alone change into her dress.

"Don't be silly. Getting ready together is half the fun."

She didn't even want to guess what the other half was

supposed to be. Carefully stepping around Alexa's long beaded train, Evie ducked behind the dressing screen and hung the garment bag from a hook in the wall. She'd no sooner zipped up the ice-blue sheath—this time without a single hitch—when Darcy Pirelli, who owned the beauty shop in town, appeared at her side.

Fifteen minutes later, Darcy stepped back with a flourish and spun Evie's chair to face the mirror. "Voila!"

Evie stared at a woman she hardly recognized. Her reflection blinked back at her with a pair of ridiculously long lashes. Her lips had been painted, her eyes smoked and her hair styled and sprayed into an updo that seemed to defy the laws of gravity.

"You look amazing."

"That's supposed to be my line," Evie protested as she looked away from the mirror to watch as Alexa made a final adjustment to her veil. Unlike many mother-to-be brides, Alexa hadn't gone with an empire waistline that would slightly camouflage her pregnancy. Instead, the long-sleeved, beaded ivory gown hugged her curves, including her belly, and she looked as glamorous and stunning as an A-list celebrity flaunting her baby bump on the red carpet. "Chance isn't going to know what hit him."

"That is the idea." Alexa's lips curved in the self-satisfied smile of a woman who knew she was loved. "Although, I may be the one holding Griffin up on the walk down the aisle once you totally knock him off his feet."

"Alexa…"

With a glance at the other bridesmaids, who were busy with final touch-ups of their own, the bride-to-be leaned close as she murmured, "Rory told me about your 'plan.'"

"Then you know this whole thing was for show."

"I know that's what you say, but I also know what I

see." Turning Evie back toward the mirror, Alexa met her gaze in the reflection. "And that is a woman in love."

Standing outside the tent as they waited for the music to change, Griffin gave Alexa's arm a slight squeeze. His old friend looked gorgeous, but more than that, she radiated happiness. "Are you sure about this? Because I have the plane ready to go if you want to make a run for it."

Alexa laughed at the ridiculous suggestion. Griffin had the feeling that if he hadn't been standing by her side, waiting for their cue, she would have already rushed the tent. Heaven help any hapless bridesmaid or flower girl who might get in her way.

"I'm marrying the man I love, the father of my child, and I can't wait." Slanting Griffin a sidelong glance, Alexa said, "I think the better question is…are *you* ready?"

"Me?"

"Ready to admit that you've fallen in love with Evie." Without giving him a chance to respond, she waved a hand and Griffin had to duck to keep from getting smacked in the face with her sweetly fragrant bouquet. "And I already know about Evie's plan, so don't give me any of that."

"If you know about Evie's plan, then you know our relationship isn't real."

"Uh-huh," Alexa said, her voice filled with disbelief. "Keep telling yourself that."

Griffin sighed. "It's what Evie keeps telling me."

His childhood friend had the nerve to grin. "It's about time you met a woman who didn't fall so easily for your charm. Good for Evie to make you work for it."

Griffin opened his mouth, but the music started up again, and he didn't have a chance to tell Alexa she was right. As they stepped inside the tent, the guests seated on either side of the lace runner rose. He heard the whispers, saw the bursts of light as the cameras flashed, but walking down the aisle, Griffin had the strangest feeling of vertigo. All the right people were there, but they were in the wrong places. He should have been standing at the front of the tent by the beaming pastor and Evie... Evie should have been the one walking toward him.

With everyone else's attention on the bride, Griffin soaked up the sight of Evie in the pale blue bridesmaid's gown. She looked coolly elegant, the ice princess she'd once accused herself of being, but he knew better. He knew the warm heart of the woman beating beneath the frosty exterior.

Evie wasn't the type of woman who would fall for his flirting. Evie was too serious, too straightforward for that. She'd cut right through to the heart of him by challenging him to go after his dream, and she had made him work to go after her.

He was rich, successful, handsome, but for Evie, none of that had been enough. For her, he had to be honest. He had to be real. And not just with her but also with himself.

As they reached the dais where Chance waited, Griffin tore his attention away from Evie to meet his best friend's knowing, amused and slightly sympathetic regard. Leaning down, he brushed his lips against Alexa's cheek. He supposed he should offer some last-second heartfelt words of wisdom, but what could he possibly say? His friend had left the shadows of the past behind to run headlong into a brilliant future. Maybe instead of giving advice, he should take it.

Are you ready to admit you're in love with Evie?

He might not be able to deny his own feelings any

longer, but admitting them to Evie? That was a different story.

With all the work Rory and Evie had put into the wedding, Griffin was certain the ceremony was as lovely and romantic as the Hillcrest House brochure promised. But somehow the moments between the words *we are gathered here today* and *you may kiss the bride* were a total blur, and the next thing he knew, the guests were rising to their feet and applauding the happy couple.

He longed to reach out as Evie walked by in a whisper of satin but knew she'd never forgive him for disrupting the ceremony. Besides, he wanted to be alone when he finally told her how he felt. He kept his attention on her as the wedding party made its way back down the aisle to form a receiving line. As if feeling the caress of his stare, she glanced back over a bare shoulder for a brief moment and the look in her eyes… He saw a light there, a glimmer that sent his already pounding heart into overdrive. A flicker of emotion that had him hoping that maybe, just maybe, their story might end with *happily-ever-after*.

He was about to join the procession when he caught sight of a man breaking away from the rest of the crowd. Broad shouldered and elegantly attired in a tailored navy suit, the man ducked out a side exit of the tent before Griffin had registered more than a quick glimpse.

But that one look had been more than enough. Swearing beneath his breath, he fought the urge to knock well-dressed wedding guests aside and leap over rows of chairs to catch up to the other man. The night air was cool and crisp as he burst out of the crowded tent.

As he started walking, jogging and then flat-out sprinting toward the hotel, the same thought pounded in time with his footfalls. *This can't be happening. This can't be happening. This can't be happening.*

The man turned at the sound of Griffin's rapid approach, one foot paused on the steps to the front porch.

"Dad," Griffin greeted him grimly, "what the hell are you doing here?"

Chapter Sixteen

Frederick James eyed Griffin with an arch look as he adjusted his cuff link. In his late fifties, with his dark blond hair starting to gray at the temples, his father was still trim and fit, though Griffin didn't know how he stayed in shape considering the long hours he spent at work.

"Well, it is Christmas—a time for family. And don't act like I'm some kind of wedding crasher, son. I was invited."

As the closest neighbor to the sprawling mansion where Alexa had grown up, he wasn't surprised Frederick had been invited. But never in a million years had Griffin guessed his father would actually attend. Hell, even if he'd been the one marrying Alexa, Griffin wasn't so sure his father would have showed. "I'm not buying it," he stated flatly.

"Buying what, exactly?"

"That you're here for the wedding and not for the hotel."

"Are you going tell me Hillcrest House still isn't for sale?"

"It isn't." Or, at least, Evie wasn't willing to sell, and that was all Griffin cared about.

"So you haven't taken this opportunity to work your way into the McClaren camp to try to change their minds?"

Everything inside him rejected his father's cold, calculating take on the time he'd spent at Hillcrest House. The time he'd spent with Evie…gaining her trust. Feeling sick, he muttered, "I haven't been working anything."

Except Evie would never believe that. Not if his father was still interested in the hotel.

"Really." His father reached into his pocket and pulled out his phone. After a few swipes, he handed the device to Griffin. A photo of him and Evie in the gazebo at the Holly and Vine event filled the screen. "Because I thought you kissing Evie McClaren might have had something to do with trying to convince her to sell."

At the sound of a rough curse, Evie stopped short on the first step onto the porch. After the past few days, she'd all but memorized the sound of Griffin's laughter, of his teasing, even of his rough whisper against her skin. She'd never heard his voice raised in anger. But she would still recognize it anywhere.

He had disappeared right after the ceremony, and Rory asked Evie to go find him for the wedding photos. Climbing the steps, she felt as though the dress's skirt was weighted down with lead rather than glittering beads and seed pearls. But her feet still carried her forward, to the side of the wraparound porch, where Griffin and another man stood face-to-face. The light from the scones along the front of the hotel didn't carry around the corner, but

Evie could still see the tension in Griffin's shoulders as he confronted the other man.

"So seducing this woman had nothing to do with the hotel?"

Seducing this woman...

Evie barely swallowed a gasp. Her short nails cut into her palms as she clenched her fists. Not again. She couldn't have been so foolish, so stupid as to fall for a man's lies again.

"No, dammit!" Griffin swore. "My relationship with Evie has nothing to do with the hotel! And as for seducing a woman into selling, that's more your style than mine."

"What is that supposed to mean?"

"You tell me, Dad."

Dad? *Dad?* The man Griffin was arguing with was Frederick James?

"It took a while for me to figure it out, but I knew there had to be something more to your interest. How else would Evelyn McClaren know where I get my charm from if you hadn't *charmed* her in the past?"

Her aunt and Frederick James? Her aunt and Griffin's *father*?

Griffin had known all along, yet hadn't said a word...

And now his father was back to—

"Evelyn McClaren turned you down all those years ago. Do you really think she's going to say yes this time?"

A chill ran down Evie's spine as the elder James declared, "I'm going to do everything in my power to make sure she does."

Evie didn't need to hear any more. Slipping silently away from the James men, she raced back to the tent, cursing the stupid strappy heels as they slid on the loose gravel path. She spotted Rory near the arched arbor as the hotel photographer tried to get the family together for a group photo.

"Did you find Griffin?"

Ignoring the question, Evie demanded, "Where's Aunt E?"

"She's—" After taking a quick glance around, Rory threw her hands up in the air. "Honestly, you'd think with my own family this would be easier! We are never going to get these pictures taken if everyone keeps running off and—is everything all right, Evie? Evie!" The frustration in her cousin's voice followed Evie as she spun away again. "Now where are you going?"

Evie swore beneath her breath. Of all the times not to have her phone with her, but the sheath-style dress lacked the practicality of pockets. She had to warn her aunt. She couldn't imagine how shocked Aunt E would be to see Frederick James. After all her aunt had been through, the last thing she needed was the emotional upheaval of that man landing back in her life and coming after Hillcrest House!

Her stomach twisted into knots as she neared the hotel. She dreaded the thought of running into Griffin or his father, but where else would her aunt be? The porch was empty, but the harsh reminder of the conversation she'd overheard lingered in the night air.

Griffin had lied to her. Lies of omission about his father knowing his aunt. About his father *seducing* her aunt. And lies told straight to her face, as he looked her in the eye and promised her his father had no interest in the hotel.

And she'd believed him. Every look, every lie. God, she was such a fool!

Do you trust me, Evie?

She *had* trusted him. Worse than that, she love—

No! Evie shut off the thought before it could finish. She didn't believe in love or happily-ever-after or magic. If she needed any further proof those things didn't exist, Griffin James had handed it right to her!

My relationship with Evie has nothing to do with the hotel!

Right. Their relationship had *everything* to do with the hotel. It had from the very beginning when she'd so stupidly thought he was trying to help her. And what had he been doing instead?

Softening her up so she wouldn't fight to keep her aunt from selling? Distracting her while his father moved in for the kill?

Evie couldn't quite figure that part out, couldn't put the pieces together, but there had to be some angle she was missing. Nothing else made sense.

But whatever their plan, she was going to put a stop to it. Thirty-five years ago, her aunt chose Hillcrest House, and Evie was going to make damn sure she made that same choice again!

Ignoring the ache in her heart, Evie yanked open one of the carved double doors. The McClaren women would stand together and tell the James men to get the hell out of their hotel.

The sparkling chandelier glittered in bright contrast to the shadowed porch outside. In the split second after Evie stopped and blinked, her eyes adjusting to the well-lit lobby, a wave of nausea hit her. She was too late.

Griffin and Frederick had moved inside, but that wasn't what had Evie frozen in dismay. She watched like a passenger in a car, seeing an accident about to happen but unable to stop it, as her aunt stepped out from the hallway leading to the ballroom.

Evie knew the moment Evelyn saw Frederick James.

Her aunt's confident step stuttered to a stop as she lifted a trembling hand and laid it over her heart. Dressed in a sequined dark blue gown, Evelyn had never looked lovelier. But the signs of her battle with cancer were still evident in her slender frame and the short, layered style of her gray hair.

What might this kind of emotional shock do to her aunt? Worry and fear battered Evie's thoughts. Forget what Griffin had done to her, she would *never* forgive him for what he was doing to her aunt!

She opened her mouth to call out her aunt's name, to let Evelyn know she wasn't alone in this, but before the words could form, Evelyn moved across the lobby toward the James men, her slow, deliberate steps on the patterned carpet not unlike a wedding march.

She didn't stop until she stood in front of Frederick James, and when she raised her hand, Evie's own palm itched with her desire to slap Griffin across the face. But Evelyn didn't hit Griffin's father. Instead, she cupped the elder James's strong jaw.

"Rick," she whispered. "I can't believe you're finally here."

Turning his head, he pressed a kiss into her palm. "It's been far too long, Lynnie."

Rick? Lynnie?
What the hell?

A strangled sound escaped Evie's throat, and Griffin turned. If she didn't know better, she would have thought he looked as stunned as she felt.

"Evie!" her aunt called out. "Come meet Griffin's father, Frederick James."

She must have moved, though she didn't know how when her mind, her entire body, felt numb. But the next thing she knew, Frederick James was reaching out to shake her hand.

The older man smiled at her warmly. "Evie, such a pleasure to meet you." Glancing to the side, he added, "My son has told me so much about you."

A sickening mix of anger and disgust swirled through Evie's stomach as she imagined those conversations. The two men slapping each other on the back as they swapped stories about seducing McClaren women. Griffin sucked in a deep breath, his shoulders stiffening, almost as if he knew what she was thinking. But that wasn't possible. If he had, he wouldn't have dared to stand so close.

"Why are you here?"

"Evie!" her aunt scolded at the blunt demand. "Rick is here for the wedding. He's a Hillcrest House guest."

"A guest?" Evie echoed. "You knew he was coming here?"

Her aunt's thin eyebrows rose in a wry look. "I didn't exactly think it was a coincidence when Griffin had shown up at Hillcrest a second time, so when he did, I called Rick. We've been talking the past few days."

With a tender smile, Frederick added, "And it's been like old times."

A faint buzzing rang in Evie's ears and she only wished the sound was louder. Loud enough to drown out the thoughts drumming relentlessly through her mind. Loud enough to block out whatever else her aunt had to say. Words that Evie could already sense she didn't want to hear.

"Frederick came to Hillcrest—" Her aunt looked at the older man.

"Thirty-five years ago," he said in response to the unasked question, the two obviously on the same wavelength and—*oh, yeah*—finishing each other's sentences.

"It was right after I had taken over running Hillcrest House full-time." Evelyn tucked a lock of hair behind her ear, the light in her eyes making her look almost as young as she must have all those decades ago. "I had such big plans and no intention of selling out to some corporate chain."

"Which you made clear by all but kicking me off the property the moment we met."

Evelyn's eyebrow rose in challenge. "Not that you let that stop you from coming around."

Frederick grinned in response, the similarities between father and son so apparent Evie couldn't bring herself to look at either man. "I'm not the type to give up easily."

"More like you'd never had anyone tell you *no* before."

The last thing Evie wanted to hear about was a moment when her aunt had told Frederick James yes. But she clung to the one hope she still had. "Obviously whatever happened thirty-five years ago, you didn't end up selling the hotel."

"No, I didn't," Evelyn admitted, her attention still on Frederick as she spoke.

"I stayed in town for weeks trying to convince you before I realized it wasn't Hillcrest House I was interested in, Lynnie." Taking her hand, Frederick vowed, "It was you."

Blinking rapidly, Evelyn gave a soft laugh. "We were a couple of fools, weren't we?"

"Young fools. Hopefully we're older and wiser now."

For a long moment, the two of them didn't speak, the silent communication somehow bridging the distance that had separated them, until Evelyn finally gave a slightly embarrassed laugh. "Enough of that for now. We'll have plenty of time to catch up."

"I'm looking forward to it," Frederick assured her.

This couldn't be happening. Her aunt… Griffin's father. It was all too much.

Completely entranced with each other, her aunt and Frederick didn't even notice as Evie all but stumbled away. Wedding guests were streaming into the lobby, laughing and smiling as they headed toward the ballroom and the reception. She fought her way against the flow, battling the surge of emotion battering her every step.

Beautiful ceremony…

So romantic…

So in love…

Evie finally managed to escape to the porch, where the cool night air chilled her heated skin and stung her eyes.

"Evie."

Her hands tightened on the carved railing as she stared unseeing over Hillcrest's softly lit grounds. "You knew," she said, her voice flat with accusation, "and you never said a word."

Moving to stand beside her, Griffin shook his head. "I didn't. After some of the things my dad and your aunt said, I suspected, but I wasn't certain."

"You lied to me."

"Evie…"

"You lied, and your father—"

"Is here because thirty-five years ago, he fell in love with your aunt! And I think—even though I know he loved my mother—I think a part of him never stopped loving Evelyn."

"No, that's not…" Evie shook her head. A love that survived for over three decades? "I don't believe it."

"It's true, Evie." Griffin flung a hand back toward the open lobby doors. "Look at them!"

But Evie didn't want to look back into the crowded

lobby, where her aunt and his father still stood, the sea of guests parting around them. Seeing the two gazing at each other hurt something deep inside her. Something that was still broken and, she feared, always would be.

"He's using her. He's using her the same way you used me."

Griffin flinched, reeling back as if she'd struck him. "Dammit, Evie, can't you see that I don't have some hidden agenda? I wasn't using you! The only thing I was doing the whole time I was here was loving you!"

Her heart clenched at the passionate declaration. She wanted to believe him. Oh, how she wanted to! But she couldn't. The last time she'd believed in love, it had ripped her apart. It had torn her away from Hillcrest House, away from her family. She hadn't been there when her aunt needed her, and she wouldn't—couldn't—let that happen again.

As if reading her mind, Griffin's stance softened. He took a step closer, closing his hands around her upper arms and turning her toward him. "Evie…I know you're afraid. I know how much Eric hurt you, but I'm not him."

No, he was Griffin James, which made this all so much more unbelievable.

If she alone wasn't enough for a man like Eric Laughlin, did she really think she'd be able to hold on to Griffin? Charming, flirtatious, gorgeous Griffin James with hotels around the world and a private jet at his disposal.

"This isn't about Eric."

"Isn't it? You trusted him and he abused that trust. And now you don't think a man could love you for who you are. For your beauty and passion. For your quick wit and even for your sharp tongue."

He was killing her. The words acted like a battering

ram against the shield around her heart. All the things she wanted to hear…

"And I don't give a damn about Hillcrest House."

"But I do!" Evie swallowed. The hotel had been her refuge, her chance for redemption, and she needed the comfort of its timeless security now more than ever. "The hotel is all I've wanted. All I've ever wanted."

"No, Evie. It's just all you think you deserve."

If his earlier words had been blows to her heart, that final, softly spoken sentence was like a slap across the face. "And you think you—you don't even *know* me if that's what you think. This was all about Hillcrest House, remember?" She let out a laugh as ragged as the edges of her control. "This whole plan to make my aunt believe we were in love—"

A soft gasp silenced Evie's words. She had been so focused on Griffin, she hadn't noticed her aunt stepping out onto the porch. Light streaming out from the lobby illuminated the confusion and hurt mingled in Evelyn's expression as she glanced between Evie and Griffin. "What do you mean, make me *believe* the two of you were in love?"

Evie's heart pounded so hard inside her chest, she almost expected the fragile strands holding the seed pearls on the bodice of her dress to snap, sending the delicate beads spilling out across the floor. The way it felt, her every emotion was threatening to pour out at Griffin's feet.

"Evie." He cupped her cheek in his hand. "No more pretending."

He stood in front of her, so serious, so…sincere. No sign of the laughing, flirting Griffin James remained. Somewhere along the way, he'd dropped that pretense, allowing her to see the *real* man inside.

A man she could trust. A man she could love…if only she could believe.

Turning to her aunt, Evie swallowed hard against the lump in her throat. She'd wanted so much for her aunt to be proud of her, to trust her with the legacy of the hotel that meant so much to both of them. To make up for the mistakes of the past when loving the wrong man had cost her the chance. "I wanted to prove to you that I could run Hillcrest and still have a life, so I came up with a plan."

Tears burned the back of her throat as she stepped out of Griffin's warm embrace and into the cold, empty night air. "A plan to fool you into thinking Griffin and I had fallen in love, but none of it was real." Not the laughter they'd shared, not the love they'd made. "And now it's over."

Griffin wasn't sure how he ended up at the gazebo. All he'd known after he left Evie on the porch was that he couldn't go into the hotel and he sure as hell wasn't going to the wedding reception. The thought of seeing Chance and Alexa together, so committed to each other, so in love, gutted him.

None of it was real…and now it's over.

He didn't know how long he sat in the darkness, the twinkling stars overhead, the sound of the waves breaking against the shore, before he caught sight of a shadow off to the left near the tree-lined pathway. The broad-shouldered form was in silhouette, but he still recognized his father.

Settling onto the step beside him, Frederick handed him a bottle of beer.

"How'd you know to find me here?"

Frederick glanced back at the gazebo with a shrug. "Just a feeling. This place has always been…special."

"Okay, no. I really don't want to hear about that."

Frederick's teeth flashed in the darkness before his smile faded. "I loved your mother, Griffin," he said, and even in the faint landscape lighting, Griffin could see the sincerity and emotion in his father's expression. "I need you to know that."

"Dad…" Shocked that his father felt he had to say the words, he insisted, "I never doubted that."

Not like Evie doubted him.

Spinning the cold bottle between his hands, he asked, "But what really happened between you and Evelyn Mc-Claren all those years ago?"

Frederick sighed. "I was young. Headstrong." He chuckled. "Almost as headstrong as Lynnie. I was just out of college and ready to make my mark on the world. I'd already taken over for your grandfather and wanted to expand James Hotels into the global market. Staying at Hillcrest House was never part of the plan."

"And now?" Griffin asked after tipping back the beer, as if the mellow brew could wash the sour taste from his mouth. "What's your plan for the hotel now?"

For a long moment, Frederick didn't speak. Finally, he said, "You know Evelyn wants to sell, right?"

"I know, but—but not to us, okay?" Losing Hillcrest to his father would ruin Evie, and even though she had already destroyed him, he cared too much to let that happen. "You can buy any other hotel in California, in the world, but not this one. Please, Dad."

"It means that much to you?" his father asked.

Griffin swallowed. "It means—" *ah, hell* "—everything to me."

"So if I agree to this," his father stated, "you'd be willing to oversee the new hotel in Japan?"

"Sure," he agreed hollowly. Why not? Maybe being

half a world away from Evie McClaren would ease the ache in his chest.

"You would do that for her?" his father asked.

"I would do anything," Griffin swore.

"Well, fortunately for you, you don't have to." Reaching into his suit jacket, Frederick pulled out an envelope and handed it to Griffin.

"What is this?"

"Consider it a Christmas present. It's the paperwork releasing your trust fund. Signed, sealed and now—" he gave a slight nod "—delivered."

"I don't—I don't understand. Why here? Why now?"

"It's something I should have done years ago, but I guess I thought if I held on to the trust fund long enough, if I made you work hard enough for it, you'd learn to love the hotel business the way your grandfather and I did."

Evie had been right, Griffin realized. His father had been holding on to the trust as a way to hold on to him.

"I know how much you love flying, and I shouldn't have kept you from following your dream. But maybe you'll take one bit of advice from a man who knows what he's talking about. No dream, no matter how big, means anything without someone to share it with."

After clapping him on the shoulder, Frederick pushed off the steps and left Griffin alone with his beer and the trust fund that he'd been counting on for over a decade.

He was free. Free to fly anywhere in the world—except for one problem. For the first time in his life, there was nowhere else Griffin wanted to be.

Chapter Seventeen

"Are you sure you're up to this tonight?"

Evie straightened her spine at the pity she saw in her cousin's expression. Did she want to make an appearance at Hillcrest House's New Year's Eve Ball? Only about as much as she wanted to walk naked through downtown Clearville.

Instead she would be wearing an elegant red gown with tiny jeweled straps and a floor-length satin skirt as she tried to pretend her heart wasn't broken.

"It's fine, Rory," she insisted as she leaned closer to the mirror in her bedroom to wipe at a fleck of mascara beneath one eye. The highlighter, shadow and a vat full of concealer had done a good job disguising the red eyes and dark circles. Evidence of the long sleepless nights since Frederick James had arrived a week before.

Evie hadn't seen Griffin since, but his dad? Good ole Frederick—or Rick, as *Lynnie* called him—was everywhere. Or more to the point, everywhere her aunt was, including at the McClaren family Christmas celebrations. Evie couldn't seem to turn around without bumping into the loving couple.

Frederick hadn't said anything about his son's disappearance, but Evie supposed that was one of the perks of being a pilot and owning his own plane. Griffin could take off at a moment's notice, nothing to hold him back, nothing to tie him down.

Evie swallowed as she turned away from her reflection. Of course, she could easily say the same. Though her aunt hadn't come out and told her so, Evie knew. With Evelyn talking about joining Frederick in Tokyo as he finalized the deal for the newest James hotel, Evie had to face the facts.

Her brilliant 4-F plan had ended in the biggest F of them all.

Failure.

She'd lost Griffin. She'd lost the hotel. She'd lost her job because there was no way she could stay at Hillcrest House once her aunt sold. Not because of what Frederick might do to the hotel, but because of what staying at the hotel would do to her. She couldn't work and live in a place where memories of Griffin would haunt her every time she turned around.

Grabbing a lacy shawl and her slim black purse from the dresser, she said, "Let's get this over with."

"Evie…"

"Please, Rory, I need to get through tonight—"

"And then what?" her cousin challenged.

And then the rest of her life stretched out before her looking pretty damn empty at the moment. "I'm going back to Portland. The firm said they would be interested in hiring me back."

"Oh, for goodness' sake! For once in your life, can you focus on something other than your job?"

"What do you want me to do, Rory? Focus on how because of me, Aunt E is selling Hillcrest House? Focus on how this is the second time I've screwed up the only thing I've ever wanted?"

"What happened with Eric was not your fault!"

"I was so stupid and so blind to the kind of man he really was. You and Chance warned me. If I'd listened, I would have been here to help Aunt E. I would have made sure she took better care of herself, that she didn't skip out on doctor's appointments and mammograms and—"

"Evie." Shocked filled Rory's voice as she sank down on the corner of the bed. "You can't really believe that Aunt E's cancer is your fault! And if you do, then doesn't that mean Chance and I are just as guilty? I've spent the past five years in LA and Chance has been living all around the world for almost a decade."

"I—" Her cousin's words stumped her for a minute before Evie shook her head. "I was the one who was supposed to take over until I fell for Eric."

"You made a mistake, Evie. We all have, and we both know Aunt E. She's as stubborn as—well, as *you* are. She wouldn't have run Hillcrest all these years unless it was what she wanted to do. Besides," Rory added, "if this is anyone's fault, it's mine."

"Yours?" Evie gave a scoffing laugh. Despite what Rory had said about everyone making mistakes, Evie still had a hard time seeing her cousin as anything other than perfect. With the perfect soon-to-be husband and perfect family.

"All my talk about Hillcrest's magic…"

As Rory's voice trailed off, Evie held up a hand and she sat beside her cousin. "Don't, okay?" Her voice broke a bit on the question. "I've had enough shocks the past week for an entire lifetime. The last thing I need right now is you telling me that you don't believe Hillcrest is magic after all."

"Of course I still believe." Reaching over, Rory took Evie's hand in hers. "Hillcrest House has always been able to bring two hearts together, a place where couples fall in love and—"

Struggling to reclaim some of her previous cynicism, Evie muttered, "Blah, blah, blah."

After making a face, Rory said, "My point is that love isn't all about magic. It's also about effort and hard work. About not giving up even when times are tough and about wanting that love to last more than anything."

Not so long ago, Evie had determined she wanted Hillcrest more than anything. She'd put together a plan and had gone to great lengths to obtain that goal. Her plan had failed, but at the moment, that wasn't the point. The point was that she'd *tried*.

But with Griffin…instead of standing and fighting, she'd run scared.

The only thing I was doing here was loving you!

She been too afraid to believe he could actually love her, so she'd pushed him away. She'd hidden behind Hillcrest and their fake relationship rather than admit her real feelings.

"All I'm saying is, don't give up on love, Evie," her cousin encouraged her.

Good advice, but too little, too late, Evie feared. Thanks to how she'd pushed him away, Griffin had already given up on her.

Though her own plan might have fallen apart, the New Year's Eve Ball had come together beautifully. The elegant walnut-paneled ballroom was packed with hotel guests and Clearville locals, most making use of the party hats and noisemakers handed out at the door. If this was to be her last event at the hotel, at least she was going out with a bang.

During a break in the music, Evie made her way toward the small stage, her legs trembling on each step. Normally, Rory would welcome the guests to the hotel, but tonight Evie was making her stand. No more running, no more hiding.

Her determination faded a bit as she reached the microphone and looked out over the well-dressed audience. She spotted several familiar faces in the crowd, many of whom had spoken their vows at Hillcrest House. Couples who'd had the courage to believe in each other and to hold on to the faith that their love would be strong enough to get them through good times and bad. Couples like Rory and Jamison, like Chance and Alexa…like her Aunt Evelyn and Frederick James.

Drawing on their courage and strength, Evie took a deep breath. "Welcome, everyone, to our New Year's Eve Ball. I hope you are all enjoying the beauty and…romance of Hillcrest House. My cousin Rory and I want to give our entire staff a huge hand for making this evening such a success. I especially want to mention our marvelous chef, Aaron, and our manager, Trisha, and to also offer them our congratulations on their recent marriage."

Though Aaron was safely back in the kitchen, enough people offered catcalls and whistles to have Trisha, standing at the back of the room, ducking her head before giving an embarrassed wave.

As the applause died down, Evie said, "I also want to thank my aunt for giving Rory and me this chance to run Hillcrest for the past several months."

Evelyn shook her head in protest, but Rory and Jamison urged her up the few steps. The applause rose, and Evie's throat ached as her aunt crossed the stage to give her a hug.

"Thank you, Evie and Rory. You've done a marvelous job in my absence, as I knew you would. You have both made me so proud." Turning to face the crowd, she said, "And now I have an announcement of my own to make. Thirty-five years ago, Frederick James asked me to marry him, and yesterday I said yes."

The cheers that had barely died down erupted once again as Evelyn called Frederick up to stand beside her. Joy radiated from the couple as Frederick swept Evelyn into his arms. Laughing and breathless once he set her back on her feet, she finished her speech. "I know many of you are probably wondering what this means for Hillcrest House, but I am confident I am leaving her in the best of hands," she said as she reached out for Frederick's. "Thank you, and enjoy the ball."

So that was it. Hillcrest was officially a James hotel.

Evie's eyes burned, and she could only hope that anyone who noticed would think they were happy tears. Because she *was* happy. As much as she longed to rush from the stage, to find some solitary corner to cry her eyes out, she refused to allow her own heartache to ruin her aunt's happiness. Her aunt deserved to live life to the fullest. And seeing Evelyn and Frederick together, it was clear. Hillcrest's magic was alive and well.

For everyone else, if not for Evie.

Those who don't believe will never bother to look.

Evie closed her eyes and the painful truth hit. She'd had love. She'd had magic. But she hadn't believed. She hadn't trusted that what she and Griffin had could last. That it could be real and true and strong enough to keep them together, no matter what distance might separate them. She'd been too afraid, too wrapped up in the past to see it.

Open your eyes, Evie.

Griffin's voice whispered through her, and she finally saw what had been in front of her the whole time. She loved Hillcrest House, but she loved Griffin more. And with her eyes finally open, the hotel's ballroom looked bigger, brighter, more beautiful than ever. So full of possibilities for a New Year...and a new start.

Stepping back toward the microphone, she said, "Let me be the first to congratulate you both. Anyone who knows me knows that I have not been the biggest believer in Hillcrest's magic. It was easier for me to pretend that it didn't exist than to admit how afraid I was that magic—that love—was meant for other people but not for me. It was too serious, too practical to trust in something so elusive until someone came along to show me how to laugh...and how to love."

For a split second, Evie's throat closed. She forgot how to breathe, how to swallow, and she was petrified that the next thing to come out of her mouth would be a heartbroken sob she would never live down. But when she would have run from the stage, she thought of Griffin, of the way he'd encouraged her to let the people around her in, to allow them to see how much she cared.

"I thought by holding on to Hillcrest House, I was holding on to my family. For decades, this has been a McClaren hotel, but this building isn't what has held my family together." Glancing first at her cousins and then at her aunt, she admitted, "Love did that. Love will always do that.

"Everyone has always said how much I take after my aunt, and I know what a compliment that is. Aunt E, all my life you've been my inspiration and I've been proud to follow in your footsteps, but I'm not waiting to be with the man I love. So if you will all excuse me, I need to tell him that!"

Evie was barely aware of the cheers going up from the crowd as she turned from the microphone. Evelyn and Frederick stepped closer, their hands still linked together, huge smiles on their faces as they exchanged a private glance.

"There's something you should know, Evie."

Looking at Frederick, Evie saw how much Griffin resembled his father and knew this was what he would look like in thirty years. But unlike Evelyn and Frederick, Evie didn't want to spend all those years apart. She wanted to spend every day with Griffin and the sooner she could call him, the better. "Frederick, if we could talk about this later…"

"Your aunt did sell the hotel to a James, but not to me."

A murmur rose from the crowd as his words were picked up by the microphone.

"I don't understand. If you didn't buy it—"

"I did."

At the sound of the familiar voice, Evie's heart leaped to her throat. She looked out over the crowd, her disbelieving gaze searching… And in the back of the room, standing in front of the carved double doors, she saw him. In a tailored tuxedo, because what else would Griffin James wear? He smiled as he cut through the crowd of people, and her heart stuttered in her chest with all the emotion she couldn't express.

Climbing the steps, he greeted first his father and then Evelyn with a hug before he turned to face Evie.

"I don't understand," she whispered.

"I thought it was time—past time," Frederick acknowledged with a wry smile, "for my son to have that inheritance of his."

His inheritance? Oh, God, he didn't!

"Griffin!" She pressed her trembling hands to her mouth to keep from crying. "You can't do this!"

He flashed her his typical cocky grin, but behind the smile Evie saw the uncertainty, the hesitation and hurt she'd caused. "Pretty sure I already did."

"You can't give up your dream for mine! Aunt E, please."

Evie looked to her aunt but the older woman merely shrugged. "You know I am a businesswoman at heart," she said, the tender look and loving hand she placed on Frederick's arm contradicting the words. "We've signed on the dotted line. The deal, as they say, is done."

After leaning forward to give Evie a kiss on the cheek, Evelyn and Frederick excused themselves to mingle with the guests—leaving Evie alone onstage with Griffin.

"I don't understand why you would do this."

"Don't you, Evie?"

His golden gaze pinned her to the spot, and hope started to bubble up inside her like the champagne fizzing in the crystal flutes the guests were raising to toast Evelyn and Frederick. She could think of only one reason, the only reason that made sense even to her logical, practical mind.

He'd done this for her. He'd done this for love…

"But to give up your dream of flying when that's all you've ever wanted?"

"I never knew what I wanted until I met you," Griffin declared. "And with you and Rory at the helm, Hillcrest House is going to be the premiere boutique hotel in Northern California. I can't think of a better service to offer your guests than chartered flights into Clearville."

"But buying Hillcrest? When you said you hated the thought of running a James hotel?"

"This isn't a James hotel. This is a *McClaren* hotel. This will always be a McClaren hotel, and I don't hate that at all. Not if it means the two of us working here together."

Cupping her face in his hands, he lowered his head. He claimed her mouth with his as if one heated kiss might succeed where thousands of words would fail. Raising his head far enough to look down at her, he vowed, "I love you, Evie, and I want to spend the rest of my life proving that to you."

The glittering chandelier overhead trembled and blurred; she blinked the tears from her eyes as someone started the countdown to midnight. Evie had heard about the gorgeous Victorian's magic all her life, but for the first time since she was a little girl, she truly believed. She might not have been looking for happily-ever-after, but she'd found it. Right there at Hillcrest House…in the arms of the man she loved.

"I love you, too, Griffin. And that love is as real and lasting and genuine as Hillcrest House's magic."

As he kissed her again, and as the noisemakers and cheers sounded all around them, Evie's heart was ready to burst with happiness. Her plan had succeeded beyond her wildest dreams—family, friends, fun, falling in love… And now she could add one final F…

Forever.

* * * * *

*Don't miss the previous books in
Hillcrest House,
Stacy Connelly's miniseries for
Harlequin Special Edition!*

**The Best Man Takes a Bride
How to Be a Blissful Bride**

*Available now, wherever Harlequin books
and ebooks are sold.*

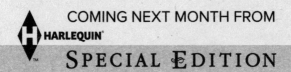
Available October 22, 2019

#2725 MAVERICK HOLIDAY MAGIC
Montana Mavericks: Six Brides for Six Brothers • by Teresa Southwick
Widowed rancher Hunter Crawford will do anything to make his daughter happy—even if it means hiring a live-in nanny he thinks he doesn't need. Merry Matthews quickly fills their house with cookies and Christmas spirit, leaving Hunter to wonder if he might be able to keep this kind of magic forever...

#2726 A WYOMING CHRISTMAS TO REMEMBER
The Wyoming Multiples • by Melissa Senate
Stricken with temporary amnesia, Maddie Wolfe can't remember a single thing about her life...or her husband, Sawyer. But even with electricity crackling between them, it turns out their fairy tale was careening toward disaster. Will a little Christmas spirit help Maddie find her memories—and the Wolfes find the spark again?

#2727 THE SCROOGE OF LOON LAKE
Small-Town Sweethearts • by Carrie Nichols
Former navy lieutenant Desmond "Des" Gallagher has only bad memories of Christmas from his childhood, so he hides away in the workshop of his barn during the holidays. But Natalie Pierce is determined to get his help to save her son's horse therapy program, and Des finds himself drawn to a woman he's not sure he can love the way she needs.

#2728 THEIR UNEXPECTED CHRISTMAS GIFT
The Stone Gap Inn • by Shirley Jump
When a baby shows up in the kitchen of a bed-and-breakfast, chef Nick Jackson helps the baby's aunt, Vivian Winthrop, create a makeshift family to give little Ellie a perfect Christmas. But playing family together might get more serious than either of them thought it could...

#2729 A DOWN-HOME SAVANNAH CHRISTMAS
The Savannah Sisters • by Nancy Robards Thompson
The odds of Ellie Clark falling for Daniel Quindlin are slim to none. First, she isn't home to stay. And second, Daniel caused Ellie's fiancé to leave her at the altar. Even if he had her best interests at heart, falling for her archnemesis just isn't natural. Well, neither is a white Christmas in Savannah...

#2730 HOLIDAY BY CANDLELIGHT
Sutter Creek, Montana • by Laurel Greer
Avalanche survivor Dr. Caleb Matsuda is intent on living a risk-free life. But planning a holiday party with free-spirited mountain rescuer Garnet James tempts the handsome doctor to take a chance on love.

Stricken with temporary amnesia, Maddie Wolfe can't remember a single thing about her life...or her husband, Sawyer. But even with electricity crackling between them, it turns out their fairy tale was careening toward disaster. Will a little Christmas spirit help Maddie find her memories—and the Wolfes find the spark again?

Read on for a sneak preview of
A Wyoming Christmas to Remember
by Melissa Senate,
the next book in the Wyoming Multiples miniseries.

"Three weeks?" she repeated. "I might not remember anything about myself for three weeks?"

Dr. Addison gave her a reassuring smile. "Could be sooner. But we'll run some tests, and based on how well you're doing now, I don't see any reason why you can't be discharged later today."

Discharged where? Where did she live?

With your husband, she reminded herself.

She bolted upright again, her gaze moving to Sawyer, who pocketed his phone and came back over, sitting down and taking her hand in both of his. "Do I—do we—have children?" she asked him. She couldn't forget her own children. She couldn't.

"No," he said, glancing away for a moment. "Your parents and Jenna will be here in fifteen minutes," he said. "They're ecstatic you're awake. I let them know you might not remember them straightaway."

"Jenna?" she asked.

"Your twin sister. You're very close. To your parents, too. Your family is incredible—very warm and loving."

That was good.

She took a deep breath and looked at her hand in his. Her left hand. She wasn't wearing a wedding ring. He wore one, though—a gold band. So where was hers?

"Why aren't I wearing a wedding ring?" she asked.

His expression changed on a dime. He looked at her, then down at his feet. Dark brown cowboy boots.

Uh-oh, she thought. *He doesn't want to tell me. What is that about?*

Two orderlies came in just then, and Dr. Addison let Maddie know it was time for her CT scan, and that by the time she was done, her family would probably be here.

"I'll be waiting right here," Sawyer said, gently cupping his hand to her cheek.

As the orderlies wheeled her toward the door, she realized she missed Sawyer—looking at him, talking to him, her hand in his, his hand on her face. That had to be a good sign, right?

Even if she wasn't wearing her ring.

Don't miss
A Wyoming Christmas to Remember
by Melissa Senate,
available November 2019 wherever
Harlequin® Special Edition books and ebooks are sold.

www.Harlequin.com

Get 4 FREE REWARDS!

We'll send you 2 FREE Books plus 2 FREE Mystery Gifts.

Harlequin® Special Edition books feature heroines finding the balance between their work life and personal life on the way to finding true love.

FREE
Value Over
$20

YES! Please send me 2 FREE Harlequin® Special Edition novels and my 2 FREE gifts (gifts are worth about $10 retail). After receiving them, if I don't wish to receive any more books, I can return the shipping statement marked "cancel." If I don't cancel, I will receive 6 brand-new novels every month and be billed just $4.99 per book in the U.S. or $5.74 per book in Canada. That's a savings of at least 12% off the cover price! It's quite a bargain! Shipping and handling is just 50¢ per book in the U.S. and $1.25 per book in Canada.* I understand that accepting the 2 free books and gifts places me under no obligation to buy anything. I can always return a shipment and cancel at any time. The free books and gifts are mine to keep no matter what I decide.

235/335 HDN GNMP

Name (please print)

Address   Apt. #

City   State/Province   Zip/Postal Code

Mail to the **Reader Service:**
IN U.S.A.: P.O. Box 1341, Buffalo, NY 14240-8531
IN CANADA: P.O. Box 603, Fort Erie, Ontario L2A 5X3

Want to try 2 free books from another series? Call 1-800-873-8635 or visit www.ReaderService.com.

SPECIAL EXCERPT FROM

HQN™

*Seven years ago, Elizabeth Hamilton ran away from
her family. Now she's back to end things permanently,
only to discover how very much she wants to stay.
Can the hurt of the past seven years be healed over
the course of one Christmas season and bring the
Hamiltons the gift of a new beginning?*

Turn the page for a sneak peek at
New York Times *bestselling author RaeAnne Thayne's
heartwarming Haven Point story*
Coming Home for Christmas, *available now!*

This was it.

Luke Hamilton waited outside the big rambling Victorian
house in a little coastal town in Oregon, hands shoved into the
pockets of his coat against the wet slap of air and the nerves
churning through him.

Elizabeth was here. After all the years when he had been
certain she was dead—that she had wandered into the mountains
somewhere that cold day seven years earlier or she had somehow
walked into the deep, unforgiving waters of Lake Haven—he
was going to see her again.

Though he had been given months to wrap his head around
the idea that his wife wasn't dead, that she was indeed living
under another name in this town by the sea, it still didn't seem
real.

How was he supposed to feel in this moment? He had no idea.
He only knew he was filled with a crazy mix of anticipation, fear
and the low fury that had been simmering inside him for months,
since the moment FBI agent Elliot Bailey had produced a piece
of paper with a name and an address.

Luke still couldn't quite believe she was in there—the wife he
had not seen in seven years. The wife who had disappeared off

PHRTEXP1019R

the face of the earth, leaving plenty of people to speculate that he had somehow hurt her, even killed her.

For all those days and months and years, he had lived with the ghost of Elizabeth Sinclair and the love they had once shared.

He was never nervous, damn it. So why did his skin itch and his stomach seethe and his hands grip the cold metal of the porch railing as if his suddenly weak knees would give way and make him topple over if he let go?

A moment later, he sensed movement inside the foyer of the house. The woman he had spoken with when he had first pulled up to this address, the woman who had been hanging Christmas lights around the big charming home and who had looked at him with such suspicion and had not invited him to wait inside, opened the door. One hand was thrust into her coat pocket around a questionable-looking bulge.

She was either concealing a handgun or a Taser or pepper spray. Since he was not familiar with the woman, Luke couldn't begin to guess which. Her features had lost none of that alert wariness that told him she would do whatever necessary to protect Elizabeth.

He wanted to tell her he would never hurt his wife, but it was a refrain he had grown tired of repeating. Over the years, he had become inured to people's opinions on the matter. Let them think what the hell they wanted. He knew the truth.

"Where is she?" he demanded.

There was a long pause, like that tension-filled moment just before the gunfight in Old West movies. He wouldn't have been surprised if tumbleweeds suddenly blew down the street.

Then, from behind the first woman, another figure stepped out onto the porch, slim and blonde and…shockingly familiar.

He stared, stunned to his bones. It was her. Not Elizabeth. *Her*. He had seen this woman around his small Idaho town of Haven Point several times over the last few years, fleeting glimpses only out of the corner of his gaze at a baseball game or a school program.

The mystery woman.

Don't miss
Coming Home for Christmas *by RaeAnne Thayne,*
available wherever
HQN books and ebooks are sold!

Looking for more satisfying love stories
with community and family at their core?

Check out **Harlequin®** **Special Edition**
and **Love Inspired®** books!

New books available every month!

CONNECT WITH US AT:

Facebook.com/groups/HarlequinConnection

 Facebook.com/HarlequinBooks

 Twitter.com/HarlequinBooks

 Instagram.com/HarlequinBooks

 Pinterest.com/HarlequinBooks

ReaderService.com

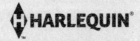

**ROMANCE WHEN
YOU NEED IT**

HFGENRE2018